MW00812385

A S

an

Dachshund in Athens

A Patricia Fisher Mystery Book 8

Steve Higgs

To anyone feeling blessed to have a sausage dog in their house. Mine are the funniest, most individual dogs I have ever known.

Contents

DEAD RELATIVE

'He's dead.'

It was a simple statement, but it encapsulated everything I needed to know very quickly. I had only met him two days ago, but he was a delightful young man with a promising future. That future had been snatched away now, apparently by his own hand.

My name is Patricia Fisher. I'm just a lady on a cruise ship, but it just happens to be the Aurelia, the world's largest and most luxurious cruise liner and by the hand of fate, I am staying in the biggest and best suite it has. I'm also dating the captain of the ship, Alistair Huntley, and I have an unwelcome habit of finding dead bodies or uncovering crimes when I would rather be sitting on a sun bed reading a trashy novel and sipping gin.

The body sitting in a desk chair with his head lying next to a computer keyboard had been found after he failed to report for work this morning. Another member of crew sent to rouse him, called for security when he got no answer and that was when they discovered his body. A trickle of blood ran from his left temple to pool on the desk and a small handgun lay discarded on the floor where it had fallen from his limp hand.

The official announcement of death was made by Dr Kim, one of the ship's doctors, though I thought it quite obvious from the poor young man's pallor that life had left him some hours ago. As Dr Kim stepped back, his task now complete, Lieutenant Martin Baker stepped into the now vacant spot next to the body. Crew cabins were small, especially for junior personnel. Julian Young was a bursar's assistant, which in layman's terms meant he was an accountant. I knew all this already because he was also the captain's nephew, his younger sister's eldest child and someone he had proudly introduced me to when I returned to the ship from Zangrabar. I think Alistair had been happy that someone else in the family wanted to follow his path. I wondered what he would think now.

Lieutenant Baker reached over the body to click the mouse which was still gripped in Julian's hand. The screen of the computer flicked to life, displaying a word document.

Lieutenant Deepa Bhukari moved to join her colleague in reading it, curiosity getting the better of me and Dr Kim as well so we joined her.

Dear Everyone,

I can no longer live with the crushing depression I suffer each day as a result of my disability. I'm sorry for the mess I leave behind for others to clear up. This is the best thing for me and for those around me. Please tell my mother that I love her.

Julian

It was a sad note and very short. It also told me that he had been murdered.

'What was his disability?' asked Deepa standing back to get some room after crowding around the screen with the rest of us. She was looking at the dead man as if trying to spot a physical abnormality.

'He was deaf,' I replied. 'He didn't see it as a disability at all which makes the authenticity of the suicide note questionable. I also know that he was right-handed.'

Both members of the security team looked at the body. 'But he shot himself with his left hand,' observed Baker, sensing what that might mean. 'This wasn't a suicide, was it?'

I pursed my lips and blew out my cheeks before I let myself make a bold statement. After a second of deliberation, I said, 'I don't think so. I met him a few hours after we got back from Zangrabar. He was pleasant to speak with and excited to meet me. He was also very excited to have a job on board his uncle's ship and couldn't stop listing all the places he was going to get to visit and all the things he was going to do. He lipread and was able to hold a conversation without the deafness being noticeable. He came on board as we got off in India, so what's that... six days? In six days, he went from happy and excited to depressed and suicidal? No, he managed to attract the attention of someone who felt the need to kill him. He was murdered, and we are going to work out who did it.'

'There's something we have to do first,' Lieutenant Baker said quietly.

'What's that?'

He sniffed deeply, the air escaping again as a sigh. 'We have to tell the captain his nephew is dead.'

A New Mystery to Solve

Alistair took the news quietly. He could tell something was wrong when he saw our faces approaching across the bridge but waited until we were alone in his private quarters before he asked Lieutenant Baker to spit it out.

He didn't argue or try to deny what he was being told. Instead, he turned around to look out the window of his cabin and stare at the endless grey ocean outside. 'Please leave me,' he said quietly. As his two officers made their way to the door, I hesitated and he turned to look at me, a single tear in his right eye. 'Please stay,' he begged as he lifted an arm in welcome. I stepped into his embrace and held him for a while.

With his heart beating against me and his chin resting on top of my head, he asked, 'Can you find the person responsible please, Patricia?'

I expected nothing less. 'Of course.' Suddenly I had a new mystery to solve; one with a personal element to it. Someone had killed Julian and I knew the full company of the ship's security team would be at my disposal in my bid to find out who and why.

We said nothing else for several minutes, both of us taking comfort in the presence and warmth of the other. Eventually though, he moved, breaking the embrace and taking a step back. 'I must return to my duties. There is much to do before we dock tonight.'

I placed a steadying hand on his arm. 'It's okay to take some time for yourself,' I told him. 'Your crew know their tasks and will make you proud.'

He nodded curtly. 'I know. However, I think it best if I keep myself busy. I don't want to dwell, and I have to work out what I am going to say when I phone my sister and her husband.'

He was probably right about distracting himself. I could only imagine how he felt right now. Julian got the job because of Alistair who admitted he had to create a post for him to occupy. He would blame himself, that much I was sure of, so now I had to prove why that was not the case.

'What about your dinner tonight? Will you cancel?' Alistair was being hosted by the mayor of Athens along with the chief of police and many other local dignitaries. He wasn't enthralled at the prospect, insisting that I not join him because it would be boring. Surely, he had a legitimate excuse to duck it now though even if it was company business.

He shook his head and went back to staring out to sea. 'I could cancel, but I would just be making an excuse. The local economy relies on the cruise ships coming in and out and Purple Star Lines relies on the captains doing their part for local relationships.'

'You have a deputy,' I argued.

He pulled me into an embrace without offering any further argument. He was all about duty, no matter the personal cost. We kissed before I left, a peck on the lips and then I left him to gather himself. Outside, I found Baker and Bhukari waiting for me in the passageway. The captain's private quarters are situated behind the bridge, high up in the superstructure to give a commanding view of the ship and to place him immediately to hand when an emergency occurred during his off-duty periods. Normally, only crew ever got to come up to the bridge, but our relationship had bent the rules a little so that I now had my own access pass to the crew-only elevator.

On the walk back to the elevator, both officers followed me. 'Where do you want to start?' asked Deepa.

'Breakfast,' I replied. 'I want to start with breakfast.' I was out for my morning jog when I saw Dr Kim hurrying with his medical bag. I knew the look on his face, so I followed him which was how I came to be there when the good doctor announced Julian's death. Whatever I had planned for today was out the window now because I had a case to crack. Breakfast was necessary though, that and a shower.

My butler Jermaine was waiting for me when I got back to my suite. I had been gone for more than an hour, far longer than usual which explained the concerned look on his face. Anna, my miniature Dachshund, barked and ran across the carpet to greet me and voice her disapproval at the two people following me in. She held back from ravaging their ankles though. Her change in aggression level was partly due to some training I performed with her and partly due to being pregnant. At least I thought she was pregnant. She found her way into a pack of Corgis in Zangrabar and had mellowed since the experience.

Jermaine crossed the suite to take hats from the two security officers. 'Good morning, Lieutenant Bhukari, good morning, Lieutenant Baker. Is everything alright, madam?' he asked as he placed their items neatly on a shelf by the main entrance.

'Um, well... yes and no,' I replied cryptically. 'We have a mystery to look into, I'm afraid. I'll leave Deepa and Martin to fill you in on the details while I get clean and dress for the day. Is there coffee?'

'Of course, madam. What may I serve you for breakfast this morning?'

'Do we have any English muffins?'

'Of course, madam. I collected them this morning while you were out. It gave me a chance to exercise Anna.'

My stomach growled hungrily at the thought. 'Then eggs Benedict, please with a side of bacon.' Baker made a small sound of interest, his mouth almost drooling when I looked. I laughed at him. 'I'm sure we have enough for everyone if you are hungry.'

Twenty minutes later, three of us were tucking into the breakfast feast, lashings of buttery Hollandaise sauce dripping down my fork where it threatened to make my hand greasy. 'Exquisite as always, Jermaine. Thank you,' I praised him as I mopped up the last piece of egg. 'Now, I fear, we must get on with our day.' Breakfast conversation had focused on Julian Young and what might have befallen him. It was too early for conjecture, but we made a list of persons to speak with and questions to ask.

Washing down the last morsels with a glass of freshly squeezed orange juice, I dabbed my mouth with a napkin and pushed back my chair. Should I take Anna with me or leave her here? She was asleep on a couch looking quite content, so I decided to leave her behind. She didn't need the exercise and might be growing puppies in there somewhere.

'Ready when you are,' I said to Deepa and Martin. Their breakfast plates were also devoid of food, both of them putting away Jermaine's creation as if famished. They were ready though and steadfastly determined to assist me in bringing the killer to justice. Despite the suicide note and well-arranged scene, I was convinced it was murder; there were too many incongruities for it to be anything else.

The question then was; why kill him? Someone had to gain from his death and now I had to find the trail of breadcrumbs that would tell me who that was and what it was that they gained. We were at ground zero though; at this point in time I knew nothing at all and had a metaphorical mountain to climb while blindfolded.

Good: I like a challenge.

Bursary

Julian worked as an assistant bursar. It was a job that Alistair had to create just so he could bring his nephew on board but also one to which his nephew was well suited. Julian trained as an accountant and spent two years honing his skills in a large firm before opting to stretch his legs and see the world.

He was a handsome man, athletic too and quite tall at somewhere close to six feet four inches. I had no knowledge of his personal life, though I felt I would need to delve into it now. He would have attracted the interest of several ladies even in his short time on board and therein may lie a motive for his death. I didn't want to get too far ahead of myself though; conjecture at this stage would do nobody any favours. Instead, I prepared my head to be a clean page, ready to make notes and observe without opinion.

We could have stayed in his cabin until they removed the body, but a team led by Lieutenant Schneider had been there to deal with cataloguing physical evidence and to go through his personal effects. We would just have been standing around waiting, but we were heading back there now, Baker conversing with Schneider via his radio.

Like most of the crew, Julian's cabin was right down in the bowels of the ship. The bottom six decks were reserved for crew accommodation, storage, engine rooms and a number of other services such as laundry. Getting there was simple enough, but it wasn't quick. One had to take an elevator to get down to deck seven and then go around to one of the crew elevators to go down to the lower, crew only, decks and then walk to the destination. The Aurelia, pride of Purple Star's fleet, was more than a thousand feet long so to get from one end to the other on foot took a while.

Finally arriving at the open door to his cabin, we found Schneider inside with several other members of the ship's security team. 'You find anything?' asked Baker on his way in.

Schneider, the tall Austrian, turned to see who it was. 'Oh, hi, Mrs Fisher. Nice to see you.'

'Yes, hello,' I replied with a wave. 'I wish we could just meet on a sun terrace for once. That might be nicer.'

He didn't argue, conceding the point with an awkward expression. Then he answered Baker's question. 'There's not much to suggest it wasn't a suicide as you suggested earlier. We found no additional fingerprints on the weapon. Not that it's hard to wipe a gun down and then put it into the victim's hand. There was no suggestion of a fight either though, or that the body might have been moved. We found no blood anywhere else so I want to believe the fatal wound was inflicted at the desk where we found him.'

'Have you swabbed for DNA?' asked Bhukari.

'It'll be done in the medical centre. It's worth doing, but if he was murdered then the killer went to some lengths to make it look like a suicide, I personally doubt they would then leave their DNA around. Besides, unless we got it from skin found under his fingernails, which is dubious because there is no sign of a struggle, then it would be circumstantial.'

I knew what he meant. If we found hair from the killer, they could claim to have bumped into him, or to have popped into his room to borrow a pen. We would need more than the ability to place a person at the scene.

'Anything interesting on his computer?' asked Lieutenant Baker.

Schneider clicked the mouse to bring the screen to life, but said, 'Not really. He was working on an account in his spare time. He was new on board of course and most likely trying to impress by putting in extra hours. You'll want someone who knows bookkeeping to have a look at it though; it's all gibberish to me.'

'This is an account for the Aurelia?' I asked, staring at the screen but having no more luck than anyone else in deciphering the numbers shown.

Schneider just shrugged. 'Probably.'

He was right about getting someone in the know to check them over; maybe there was something in the numbers that would explain why he was dead. 'I need a copy of the files.' I had a thumb drive data storage device somewhere in my handbag. I had to root around to find it, eventually digging it out of its hiding place beneath a tube of hand cream. Schneider accepted it from me and plugged it in as I used the hand cream to moisturise my dry fingers and palms.

'Can I get a squirt?' asked Deepa Bhukari, the men wisely saying nothing as the only two ladies in the room stayed ahead of their beauty regimes.

Schneider handed the thumb drive back. 'I gave you everything from his computer; there really wasn't much on it but it looks new so he might have only just bought it.' I thanked him and thought about what else we might need to see before we moved on. I couldn't come up with anything immediately, so I thanked him and asked that he let us know if his search of the cabin turned up anything interesting.

Out in the passageway and heading back the way we came, Baker asked, 'Where to next, boss?'

I only had one destination in mind: the bursary. Julian worked there, and in all likelihood, he was killed by someone who knew him. His work colleagues would know his movements and habits, who he spoke with and perhaps even what he did in his down time. I would also find his boss there, the bursar, who was someone I expected to be able tell us what he was working on and why.

I hadn't met the bursar yet. Not that I was aware of anyway, so I asked Baker and Bhukari about him as we travelled upwards again in the elevator.

'Commander Krill? He's nice enough,' said Deepa, frowning a little as she said it. Eyeing her, I teased a little more out without having to say anything. 'He could do with some hygiene lessons.' When I continued to look at her, she said, 'He smells. He gets called Stinky Pete because, well because he has body odour and... well actually his first name is William. Unfortunately, he also thinks people like him, so he comes and talks to them.'

'He's never talked to me,' argued Baker. 'Not once. Ever.'

'You think it's just women he talks to?' she questioned in return, not challenging him, but seeking his opinion.

He thought about it before answering, but said, 'I couldn't say. I just know he has never spoken to me and we have been in the same room plenty of times. You're right about the body odour though. He gets halitosis too from what I hear; breath that could strip paint.'

Right. Wow. That painted a clear picture. I wasn't looking forward to meeting him anymore, but it was a task I had to perform whether I wanted to or not.

The bursary was situated on deck ten toward the stern of the ship, which made me wonder whose job it was to decide where different functions get located. Deck ten was mostly passenger accommodation. There were no sun decks or shops or even restaurants this far down into the ship so the bits that weren't accommodation were service rooms dedicated to vital functions such as water or electricity and… the bursary.

I found the bursar's office easily enough because my two companions knew exactly where it was. The outer door was locked but an intercom panel next to it put Lieutenant Baker in contact with a person inside. The conversation took seconds and the door buzzed open. 'After you,' Baker held the door for Bhukari and me to enter then followed us inside.

It looked like an office anywhere on the planet by which I mean it was mostly open plan with two glass cubicle offices at the far end for the more senior persons to work in private. Where the desks were arranged in blocks, they had photographs and postcards or little mementos, plus trinkets and other personal effects dotted in between files and folders and their computers. I had never worked in an office but I'd visited friends who did and seen things on television that caused me to believe what I was looking at now was typical.

The bursar, who I now recognised from formal parties, was approaching us with a big smile on his face. Did he not know? 'Welcome, welcome,' he gushed, shaking my hand first and then also those of both security officers. 'We so rarely get any visitors in here.' Then his smile dropped as if he just remembered why we were visiting. 'Of course, I wish it were under more joyous circumstances. Terrible business. Can you tell me what happened? All I know so far is that he was found dead this morning. I don't want to jump to any conclusions, but Rick said it looked like a suicide.'

'Who is Rick?' I asked.

It was Deepa Bhukari who answered. 'Ensign Rick Rodriguez. He was sent to fetch Ensign Young from his cabin when he failed to report for work this morning. That's right, isn't it, Commander?' When she addressed him by his rank, I glanced at his epaulette. He was indeed a commander, one of the highest-ranking officers on the ship then, which perhaps indicated the vital and perhaps difficult nature of his role.

Now I was stuck with a tricky decision. If we played along and stuck to the suicide story, the killer, assuming that person was listening, would relax and perhaps go back to doing whatever nefarious thing they were doing. That might help us to catch them. However, if I argued that it was murder, the killer might panic, do something stupid and reveal themselves. I wouldn't know which strategy was the better until I chose one and got to the end of the case.

Flipping a coin in my head, I picked a route and said, 'It is too early to draw any conclusions at this time. That's why we are here actually; we have some questions to ask you. And some for your staff too.'

'Of course. Of course. We will do everything we can to help.' Behind him, all the other crew working in the bursary were watching us, their expressions varied. One young woman looked ready to cry, others looked bored, as if we were intruding on their day and should stop wasting their time.

My gut told me one of them would turn out to be the killer. Looking at them now, I figured solving the case was going to be easy.

Interviews

We started with the bursar, taking him into his private office where he assured us we could not be overheard. He was happy to answer any questions we posed, often supplying far more information than we required. Lieutenant Bhukari hadn't been wrong about his hygiene though. Trapped in the confines of his office, the pungency of his underarms began to seep into my nostrils. It made me want to round the interview up and be finished but this was too important.

'He was a great new member of staff,' the bursar said for perhaps the tenth time. 'It was early days, of course, but he was so keen, and he really knew his stuff. And he got so much done. I couldn't believe how productive he was compared to some of the others. I think a few noses got put out of joint when I made a comment about it actually.' He put a hand to his head. 'Oh, my. Is that why he killed himself? Were the others picking on him for being a brown-nosing nerd or something?'

I dismissed his question because I had a new one of my own. 'You said he was very productive. Did you not know he was taking his work back to his cabin with him to work on in his own time?'

The bursar blinked a couple of times, staring at me as if he hadn't understood what I had just said. 'Taking work back to his cabin? You mean copies of the ship's accounts?'

I wasn't sure, but I said, 'I think so. On his computer were profit and loss statements and cashflow balances. At least, that's what they looked like. I think that's the answer to how he was being so productive.'

'Yes, that would make sense. I encouraged all the staff to work hard. Sometimes meeting deadlines meant having to work extra hours.' Even though I didn't want to jump to conclusions, I was already telling myself the accounts he had on his computer had to be the key to the case. Something about them had cost him his life.

I switched tack. 'How was he socially? Did he go for a beer with the guys after his shift? Was he friendly with any of the girls?'

I caught him off balance with the change in direction, but dutifully he answered once again, shaking his head to clear it before saying, 'He was a gym lover. Surely you must have known that just by looking at him. If he ever drank beer it wasn't very often, but I don't think he went anywhere with anyone in the few days he was here. I don't know about girls either, although I will say that I think Annette was sweet for him.'

'Which one is Annette?' I asked, turning slightly so I could see out toward the office floor. 'Don't point,' I requested hastily. 'Just describe her.'

'The brunette with the short hair and the big nose.'

Okay, it wasn't a very nice way to describe her, but I knew instantly which one of the girls he was talking about, so I let it slide. 'How many women work here?'

'Only three. Annette, Shaniqua, and Shannon.'

I didn't want to guess but I did want to form as complete a picture as possible, so I nodded towards one woman who was lounging by the coffee machine. 'Who is the tall blonde woman?'

'That's Shannon,' he replied without having to look. He actually sounded proud when he said it, as if she were his daughter or something. The age gap was too small for that to be the case and he clearly wasn't her lover; people referred to him as Stinky Pete and she was a woman who clearly took pride in her appearance.

I filed the information away for later reference should it prove of interest and asked another question. 'Why do you think he would take his own life?'

Again I caught him by surprise by my switch in direction. He flapped his lips this time; open and closed like a fish as he fought for an answer. 'I don't know,' he blurted in the end. 'I can't explain it.'

Neither could I but then I was already convinced he had been murdered.

Closing my notebook and clicking the end of my pen to retract the ball, I saw the relief wash over his face. 'Thank you, Commander. We need to ask some questions of your staff as well. I think it best if we take them out of here to do that though.'

'Yes, yes, of course.' The commander was on his feet already, anxious to get out from under the spotlight. 'I, um... will you please excuse me.' He paused. 'I assume we have finished?'

'Thank you, yes,' I replied with a nod, letting him go. He rushed from the room and out of the bursary front door, leaving his staff to fend for themselves.

Lieutenant Bhukari turned to me. 'Surely we had more we needed to ask him. Why did you let him go?'

'Did you see how nervous he was getting? He is hiding something, something to do with the accounts and how they are managed. It might be nothing to do with Julian's murder and it might be everything. I just don't know what it was that had him so worried. I think we should quiz a few of the staff and maybe work out what the bursar is up to.'

The rest of the morning got eaten up by asking the same questions over and over again. Lieutenant Baker got on his radio just after the bursar left and found us an empty cabin just a short walk from the bursary. It was a quiet and comfortable place to take them to discuss what they knew about Julian and his habits. Our approach was friendly, and we took the stance that the circumstances of his death were unclear.

We didn't learn much though. Julian had been quiet, which given that he was deaf wasn't all that surprising. He would share a few words at the coffee pot like people do in millions of offices around the world, but otherwise he appeared diligent about getting his work done.

By the time we got to Annette, my stomach was starting to rumble its emptiness. It was gone noon but finally we found someone who was bothered about Julian's death. She was in love with him. Okay, love was probably too strong of a word but at twenty she was still young enough to feel her emotions tug her unexpectedly one way or another and she had been smitten by the handsome, athletic man. That he was deaf didn't bother her at all.

Not that I thought it should, but when I asked her about it, she said, 'Oh, I think it gave him a mysterious edge. He was studious and there was no chance I would be one of those girlfriends who complains that her boyfriend never listens to her, right?' She smiled at her own joke. 'He was just really nice. Not just to look at, but I think he was a nice person. He didn't notice me though; he liked Shannon.'

'Oh? Were they dating?' I asked while I made a note.

'Goodness no. Shannon doesn't date anyone. At least not that I know of.'

'Are you friends?' Lieutenant Bhukari wanted to know.

Annette's attention swung to look at Deepa's face, her own face breaking into a big grin like that question was a joke. 'Miss Untouchable? No. None of us are friends with her. She swans around the office doing whatever she wants, hardly doing any work and the bursar never says anything about it. I don't think she would bother being friendly with someone as junior as me.'

'Why is that?' Deepa persisted.

'I don't think she sees the need. She… how can I put this? She has the bursar eating out of her hand. She is tall and pretty and most of the men are happy for her to flirt a little and get away with doing next to no work.'

I was becoming interested in the office dynamics now. Something about the interplay between different people was odd. I asked Annette a question, 'But you said she doesn't date any of them. Is she gay?'

'Not that I know of,' Annette replied with a questioning look on her face as if the idea had never occurred to her before. 'She never takes any interest in the women. Not that she takes much interest in the men either; just enough to get them to do what she wants.'

Annette's interest in Julian seemed harmless enough; I got no vibe from her that she was upset at his lack of reciprocation or his interest in Shannon and she knew nothing about the accounts he was working on or what his end goal with them might be. There were still other bursary staff to talk to, but we were more than halfway through them and were thus far yet to learn anything interesting. No one came across as nervous to be interviewed. No one looked or acted guilty. Yet.

As we broke for lunch and Lieutenant Baker locked up the cabin behind us, he asked, 'Could it have been a passenger, do you think?'

He was just making conversation rather than genuinely posing a question. I answered anyway. 'There's no way of knowing yet but it feels less likely. His murder was too well planned to have been spontaneous. The killer took their time, crafting a suicide note but not leaving their own prints on the keyboard so this was no crime of passion. Our killer is someone meticulous.'

'Someone like an accountant,' Deepa commented. Then she posed a question. 'Who will you get to look at the accounts he was working on? You can't show it to any of the bursary staff, and they are the only ones on board who would be able to spot anything out of the ordinary.'

I had been thinking about that little conundrum since I took the file. Deepa had it right; the only people who would know what they were looking at were also the ones most closely connected to the victim and the group most likely to contain his killer. Who else could I take it to? There might be qualified accountants on board as passengers, but this was their holiday and I expected there to be some sensitive data in the accounts which the cruise line would not want shared with their customers. We were due to dock in Athens tonight, which brought its own set of problems, but perhaps I could find a firm there who would be able to perform a quick analysis.

Then, because Deepa had asked the question and forced me to think about it again, the answer came to me: I was going to ask Charlie.

Sweat and Tears

My security escorts left me when we got back to the top deck; they would seek out their own lunch and find me again in an hour. I returned to my suite, where my Dachshund was probably happy to see me but couldn't find the effort required to get off the couch and show it. She managed to open her eyes, scrutinising me as she tried to judge the likelihood that I was going to offer her food and then closed them again when I failed to walk toward the kitchen.

Jermaine appeared from his adjoining cabin. 'How was your morning, madam?'

'Largely unproductive, I'm afraid. We asked a lot of questions but so far all I have is more questions.' I dropped my handbag on the coffee table and settled next to my dog. 'Has she moved at all this morning?' I asked.

He came through from the kitchen to join me in the living area. 'I do not believe so, madam. She appears to be nesting already.'

'Would she do that this quickly?'

'I couldn't say, madam. That is however what her behaviour would indicate. She stole my teddy bear earlier and was quite put out when I took it back. I found her sitting on it. May I prepare a beverage for you?'

'Some sparkling water with fruit slices, please. I think I might use my lunch break to get in a quick workout. I still feel sluggish after all the fine eating and lack of exercise in Zangrabar last week.'

'I shall make it up in your sports bottle. Your gym wear is clean, folded, pressed and put away.'

'Thank you, Jermaine. You are too good to me.'

'Not at all, madam.' He paced slowly back to the kitchen where I could hear him taking items from the refrigerator.

'How are you feeling, little girl?' I asked Anna, picking her up for a cuddle. Only a few days had gone by, but a Dachshund's gestation period was eight weeks, so it made sense that she was already starting to expand. 'How many do you have in there?' I asked her, getting a lick on my chin in response.

She looked quite content sleeping on the couch, so I placed her back in the warm spot she had been snuggled into and left to get changed. A quick workout would blow out a few cobwebs and set me up nicely for the rest of the day; no mid-afternoon slump for me, the exercise would reenergise me.

Yeah. I was always telling myself silly things like that. I munched a protein bar on my way to the exclusive upper deck gymnasium. Two months ago, I met Barbara Berkeley there when I foolishly told myself I needed to lose weight and win back my husband. Charlie, my cheating, good for nothing spouse of thirty years, soon got kicked to the curb as I realised I didn't need him and that trying to lose weight for anyone other than myself was a fool's errand. Once I got that straight in my head, my life changed completely and Barbara (Barbie) Berkeley had been a part of that. Certainly she had helped me get back some of my dwindling fitness and strength, teaching me how to push my limits so that my limits extended. I had no regrets but I will admit that every time I walked to the gym I felt a sense of growing dread for the pain she was about to inflict and every time I walked back to my suite from the gym, I had to use a wall to keep myself upright.

'Hi, Patty,' she hallooed as I pushed my way through the gym door. 'I thought I wouldn't see you today? You said you were going for a run this morning.'

'Did you hear about the young bursar?'

She pushed her near-permanent smile from her face. 'Yeah. I heard it was suicide. Why would he do that?'

'He didn't. Anyway, that's what happened to my run. I got about halfway around and then saw Dr Kim. I followed him, found Martin and Deepa and... well, he was the captain's nephew, so I am trying to work out what happened to him and why.'

'You think he was murdered,' she said it as a statement, no hint of surprise in her voice.

'Yes. I just need to work out why. That's not what I came here for though.'

'No,' she grinned. 'You came here to feel powerful. Let's go.' I didn't like the look of her grin, it had far too much gleeful malice in it. I soon found out why.

Inside the gym, she had laid out a series of stations. She had a class in an hour, some seriously fit people coming to test themselves, but she figured I could use it first and set a benchmark. There were ten stations, the victims (she said athletes, but I knew better) would each pick a place to start and would then go from place to place, performing the exercise at that station. Some were bodyweight exercises such as burpees while others involved lifting weights.

I lasted for twenty minutes which I considered a victory because it was all I had time for. Finishing my third round, I collapsed onto a soft mat and wondered if I was having a heart attack.

'Well done, Patty. That was really good for an older woman.' I knew she was just trying to motivate me but I sucked in a deep breath so I could speak, 'I hate you, Barbie.' She just laughed at me.

Then she changed the subject and asked me a question. 'Do you have plans to explore tonight?' The ship would be in Athens and it would be my first time in Greece. Of course, on this voyage it had been my first time visiting everywhere the ship went. I also had no idea if I would ever be back so missing the chance to see it at night would be disappointing. I felt committed to chasing down Julian's killer though. How could I tell Alistair I hadn't caught him when I was goofing off as a tourist? 'Hideki and I are going to find somewhere nice for dinner and he booked us into a hotel for the night as he has to fly home in a few days. I wondered if you and Jermaine might join us if you didn't already have something arranged?'

It was no surprise that she wanted to spend time with Hideki. 'You like him, don't you?' I said.

She took a moment to frame her answer. 'He gets me. Most guys just want to fool about but Hideki is serious about his career and I think he would be serious about me if we could spend more time together.'

There was something she wasn't saying. I prompted her, 'What are you thinking?'

'He finds out where he will spend his junior year shortly. In about a week or so. He applied to hospitals in America mostly but also a couple in England and Australia and a few in Japan just in case. If he gets one in the states, I could find a job nearby and we could give it a go.'

'Is that what you want?'

She shrugged. 'I wanted to travel. To see the world and explore. I don't feel like I am done with that but if he is the one…'

'You have to do what is right for you.' I wasn't one to give advice on relationships. I could probably learn more from her than she could from me, but I often found myself thinking of her as the daughter I never had, and I wanted the best for her. I liked Hideki, I had from the very start but the two of them had only spent a few days together.

'What about you and the captain?' she asked suddenly, changing the focus back to me. 'What will you do when we get back to England?'

'I'm getting off. I don't know what that will mean for us as a couple, but I think it will mean it comes to an end.'

Barbie looked surprised. 'Really? Don't you want to continue seeing him?'

I sighed. Trying to balance this equation had been plaguing my thoughts for a long while. 'He is the captain of a cruise liner. This ship, his job, it is not only his career but his entire way of life. Do you know he first got a job with Purple Star when he was seventeen? He was a porter. He moved between jobs and studied in his spare time, amassing suitable qualifications and working his way up. I doubt he would leave unless compelled to do so and he wouldn't be happy anywhere else.'

'You could stay,' she said quietly.

I shook my head slowly. 'No. This cruise has been amazing. There's been a little more excitement and murder than I expected.' We both chuckled. 'But I got on this ship to escape a situation. At the time, I needed to get a few things out of my system. Now though, it's time to go home, get a divorce and forge a new life for myself.'

Barbie looked sad. 'I thought maybe you would move into the captain's quarters and become a permanent resident.'

I smiled at the notion. 'He asked, actually. I didn't give him my answer yet, but I know what it is.'

Her eyebrows rose to the top of her head as she contemplated what that meant. 'Well, that makes my decision easier. If Hideki gets a first year placement at a hospital in the states, I am going home. If he wants me to, that is. I'll be too sad staying here when you are gone.' Then she shook her head to break her train of thought and hit me with another big smile. 'So anyway, what about tonight?'

Charlie

I knew Barbie's plans for the evening, which meant I could catch up with her if the chance presented itself. It would be nice to have a dinner out with Jermaine on shore even if I didn't take Barbie up on her offer. Alistair would be stuck at a formal dinner until very late so I wouldn't see him at any point, and I doubted he would be in the mood for company once he returned to the ship after midnight.

Checking my watch told me I had fifteen minutes left to get a quick shower, snag a snack and head back to find Baker and

Bhukari for round two of the interviews. First though, I was going to call Charlie. I put it off earlier because I worried he might suck all the energy out of me before my workout. Now my exercise for the day was done, I had the added benefit of feeling powerful when I spoke to him.

I asked Jermaine to make me a sandwich, my body now in calorie deficit and ready for some carbs, then I popped the thumb drive containing Julian's files into the computer and brought up my emails. Finally, with a sigh of resignation, I called my husband.

He picked up on the second ring. 'Patricia?' his voice sounded guarded and suspicious, like he had been doing something he shouldn't and worried I could somehow see him doing it. I could imagine him glancing around now for a camera.

'Hello, Charlie. You're probably wondering why I am calling.' I didn't waste time asking about his health or the weather. 'I need a favour.'

He almost choked at the other end. 'You have got to be kidding, Patricia.'

'Aren't you going to ask me what it is?'

I could hear him grumbling to himself before he conceded. 'Okay, what is it?'

'I've just sent you an email. There's an attachment on it.'

'I have it. It's... it's accounts. A set of books for an account. Why are you sending me this?'

He was hooked, I knew he would be. 'I need someone independent to take a look at them, someone with an expert eye and decades in the business who will be able to spot an anomaly.'

'Haven't you got someone there that can do it?' he whined.

Good old Charlie. He was going to do it anyway, but not until after he had done his best to make me feel bad about asking. 'These may be linked to a crime and if they are, the criminal is most likely one of the persons from the ship's account department. Can you do it?'

'Yes, yes, of course,' he snapped irritably. 'I saw you on television, you know. Everyone did. People at work are asking me why you are on a cruise and attending a sultan's coronation while I am here in England.'

'He's a Maharaja,' I corrected him, 'and why would they ask you?' Then it dawned on me. With a gasp, I said, 'You haven't told anyone yet, have you?' I knew I was right when he refused to answer. 'Charlie I am not coming back to you. I thought I made that clear.'

'I don't want you back,' he snapped. 'I thought I made that clear. I reject you, Patricia. I will have your clothes and possessions boxed up by the time you return. I hope you saved a little bit of the money you took because you will need to rent a place to stay.'

I was starting to think calling him had been a mistake. I wanted him to perform a simple task that would take him no time at all, but somehow we were fighting about our divorce instead. I forced myself to take a deep breath. 'Charlie, you can have the house. When I get back I will find my own place to stay.' I wasn't sure how yet, but I would work out the details later. 'Can you look at that set of accounts for me, please?'

Defeated by my calmness, he had little option but to say yes or choose to be even pettier than usual. As I hung up the phone with a promise to call him back later, Jermaine delivered my sandwich and I hungrily took a bite.

I wanted to say something cutting about men, but it was just Jermaine and me in my suite and he was the loveliest man I had ever met. To make conversation for a moment, I asked, 'Do you have a plan for the evening? Have you ever been to Greece?'

He relaxed for a moment to converse with me. 'I am rather fond of Greek food. Their gyros platters are both filling and tasty so I thought I might venture out for dinner if you have no need of me.'

'Do you have someone to go with?' He looked surprised at the question. 'Barbie invited us, but I think we should let her and Hideki spend their brief time together alone and Alistair is at a formal dinner. Besides, I can't think of anyone I would rather explore Athens with.'

My butler smiled and agreed, and we made a date of it though I forced him to promise that he would ditch the butler's tails and dress like a normal person before he left the ship.

No Clues

'Can you repeat that?' Lieutenant Baker asked, beating me to the punch. We were sitting down with Lieutenant Commander Pilar Singh. He was the next most senior person in the bursary after the bursar himself. According to him, when the captain introduced Julian to their team, the bursar assigned him work by lightening everyone else's load. Martin asked the deputy bursar about the account Julian was working on. We already knew it had been given to him and who had been working it previously, so our line of questioning was designed to probe people and make sure they were telling us the truth. According to the deputy bursar, the load lightening went down well, with one exception. Another young, go-getter was most put out by having one of his accounts transferred. He made quite a fuss about it, in fact, requesting the decision be overruled.

'Any idea why he got so upset?' I asked when he finished explaining it again.

Pilar switched his gaze to look at me. 'I asked him actually. Took him to one side to make him calm down and then quizzed him on the subject. He was embarrassed about his outburst once I got him to reflect on his behaviour and he claimed he was just keen to do well, to shine above his peers and couldn't do that if we took away his work. Apparently, the account hadn't been well maintained before he took it on, and the books were all beautifully organised now. He was upset about his hard work going to someone else. It was petty stuff. I didn't say that though. I found some words of wisdom about his career instead, told him the cream always rises; that sort of thing.'

I slumped a little back into my chair. For a moment I thought we had an interesting lead, but having followed it, now it sounded like nothing more than posturing and machismo. Pilar was an easy man to talk to, his demeanour engaging and likeable and he had eyes that clearly took in more than I think others realised because he seemed to know all about the relationships and interplays within the office. None of it meant anything until he got to Shannon. 'Julian invited her out for dinner,' he told us.

I shook my head in bafflement. 'How come no one else knows that?' I asked.

'I couldn't say,' he replied. 'But I heard him. I think he caught her looking at his arms. He was one of those guys that spent a lot of time at the gym and bore the fruits of his labour. It was harmless enough; "Would you like to get dinner sometime?" I think he suggested they go ashore together in Greece if she didn't have other plans but left it open for her.'

'And what happened?'

'She knocked him back instantly. It was fairly brutal actually. I think she said, "I don't date boys." I can't be sure because I wasn't deliberately eavesdropping. I just happened to be at the coffee machine when he approached her at the photocopier.'

Lieutenant Baker jumped in with a question. 'Who does she date, sir?'

The lieutenant commander had no answer for him though. 'I don't know that I have ever seen her with anyone.' Lieutenant Baker had provided personnel files for all the crew working in the bursary. Lieutenant Bhukari handed me Shannon's file now, open on the first page with her finger pointing to a single box. It was her date of birth. I did some quick math: she was twenty-three years old, the same age as Julian so why had she turned him down and called him a boy? There could be a million reasons of course, attraction isn't as simple as finding someone pretty to look at. It was making the back of my skull itch though.

Thankfully, she was the next person to interview. After thanking the deputy bursar for his time, Lieutenant Bhukari let him out but closed the door so we could discuss what we had learned. 'Pil's a really nice guy, don't you think?' she said as she retook her seat.

'Pil?' I was confused for a second. 'Oh, you mean Pilar?' It always struck me as odd that people insisted on shortening names. Everyone always called me

Patricia, except Barbie, of course. She was the one exception. 'Yes, he came across as helpful and pleasant. I wonder if that should worry us.'

'Everyone's a suspect,' chimed Martin. 'Ensign Gosnell sounded a bit excitable.'

I pursed my lips as I considered him. 'We have yet to meet him so we can ask a few other people about it. I want to say it sounds like a storm in a teacup though.'

'Shall we move on?' asked Deepa, poised to invite the next member of the bursar team in. There was nothing else to discuss immediately. I felt that we were starting to build up a picture of the dynamics in the office, but nothing yet was surprising or interesting. Perhaps the next character would expose a juicy secret.

Lieutenant Shannon Scott hailed from Pennsylvania. I had a look at her file while Deepa settled her and performed preliminary tasks. She certainly was attractive, her heritage Scandinavian possibly, with her natural almost white-blonde hair. She was tall too at somewhere close to six feet.

'Why did you turn Julian down when he asked you out on a date?' I asked.

I caught her off guard and got to watch as her cheeks blushed bright red. 'I, ah... I.' She stopped, narrowed her lips and started again. 'I didn't think it was appropriate to get involved with a junior member of staff within my own department. It would have been unprofessional, so I stamped a lid on his advance quickly.'

It was a good answer, whether concocted on the spot or the truth, it provided a clear and completely reasonable explanation for her actions. There was something off about her though; I couldn't shift the feeling that she was hiding something; a bit like the bursar earlier.

To challenge her, I said, 'Have you ever had a relationship with a member of the crew? There's no rule against it provided the relationship is declared.'

She flicked her hair to hide her discomfort but piercing blue eyes settled on mine as she levelled a cold stare at me. 'My private life is exactly that. You have no right to ask about it unless you can show me why it might connect me to Ensign Young's death.'

She was reluctant to answer our questions, which set her apart from almost everyone else we had met today. Most of the crew were very open – they just had nothing interesting to tell us. We persisted, asking her about the staff, their relationships with the deceased and whether she had witnessed any ill-feeling toward him at any point. The trend soon became clear; she would answer questions provided they were not about her. We had been going for more than two hours when Deepa asked her what she thought about Ensign

Gosnell asking to have the pension account back.

She shook her head as if confused, then finally told us something which made us pay attention. 'Ensign Gosnell was upset about losing the pension account, but he didn't ask the bursar to give it back, Pil did.'

I needed to make sure I had this straight. 'You're saying the deputy bursar requested Commander Krill overturn his decision on reassigning the accounts to give Ensign Young work?'

'Yes. I was in the bursar's office during the whole conversation.'

Martin probed a little deeper. 'Could he have been making the request on behalf of Ensign Gosnell? Lieutenant

Commander Singh claimed that Ensign Gosnell approached him regarding the matter.'

She considered the question for a moment. 'Possibly. I don't think so, though.'

'Why is that?' he pressed. 'And why was the bursar so reluctant to reverse the decision if his deputy requested it?'

Haughtily, she looked down her nose at the security officer. 'The commander doesn't need to explain his decisions. Does the captain reverse his commands because a subordinate challenges them? As for whether Pil was asking for Gosnell, he might have been, my gut tells me he wasn't though.'

We continued our back and forth with her for a while longer. Getting nothing new that appeared helpful, other than that the deputy bursar had lied to us. Or, at least, that appeared to be the case. So now we needed to work out why.

Most of the afternoon got absorbed just like the morning had and my bottom was going numb from all the sitting around. The cabin Lieutenant Baker found us, was on the starboard side of the ship with a small porthole window looking out. Through it I had been able to see our approach to Athens as the Greek coast washed by outside. The sun beat down to make the countryside look inviting and I couldn't help the feeling that I was missing out being stuck below decks when I should be on a sun terrace somewhere soaking up vitamin D and lost in a book.

When the last member of the bursary staff left the room and it was just the three of us, I got up to stretch out my back. Deepa Bhukari said, 'I don't feel like we got much out of today.'

Martin Baker checked over his notes, shaking his head sadly. 'There's no smoking gun, that's for sure. No miraculously intuitive guess, Mrs Fisher?' he asked.

'Sadly not. Shannon Scott seemed to be offended by Ensign Young's proposition as if he were beneath her. I get her point about not dating colleagues or subordinates but there's no actual rule to stop her and why not just say that to him? Annette came across as too upset as well. It wasn't as if she was the dumped girlfriend or a one-night stand that felt rejected. She just met him but came across as deeply infatuated. The bursar was odd too. Did you both feel that about him?'

Martin nodded. 'He did seem overly keen to get away from any further questions.'

'Yes. He did,' I agreed. 'He's hiding something.'

I went through my mental checklist. 'I think we can narrow this down to three probables. The bursar is hiding something, the deputy bursar lied about Ensign Gosnell wanting the pension account back or he didn't, in which case Lieutenant Scott is lying about him. My instinct tells me Julian's death is something to do with the pension account.'

Deepa asked, 'What about,' she checked her notes, 'Ensign Steven Gosnell? The one who had the pension account before Ensign Young and then supposedly got upset about it being taken away from him? Any mileage with that?' I pursed my lips. I didn't know. It was entirely possible that the killer wasn't one of the crew from the bursary, which would mean we had wasted a day.

Martin picked up on what I was thinking. 'You know, if it's a passenger, they might get off shortly and be gone forever.' It was a troubling thought but not one I could do much about. I could hardly ask the captain to hold the ship at anchor offshore until I was able to solve the case.

'Are you both going ashore tonight?' I asked, a few ideas forming in my head.

'Only to get something to eat,' said Martin. 'This is my twelfth visit to Athens. There's this great little place a couple of streets over from the docks...'

I cut him off before he could tell me any more, 'I think we should split up and follow a few people.'

'Who?' they both asked together.

TAIL

'Yeah, who?' asked Barbie. I had not intended to involve her and Hideki but as Jermaine and I made our way to the ship's crew exit we crossed paths with them, my tall butler hard to miss. We had to get out ahead of the people we wanted to follow or risk missing them leave. Not that we could be certain they were even going ashore. Like Martin, if they had been on the ship for some time, it was likely they were bored of seeing the same places.

To get around this, Deepa and Martin remained in the crew accommodation area below decks, strategically placed so they could report on movements. My phone beeped and everyone gathered around it as I tapped the icon to open the message.

It was from Martin. 'The bursar is dressed for a night out and heading for the elevator.'

'Tell me why we are watching the bursar again,' Hideki asked. He and Barbie were holding hands, looking very much like young lovers as we all waited in the shadows of the quayside and watched the people funnelling off the ship. He was right to ask because I hadn't actually told them anything yet. Only Jermaine knew why because he had listened to my most recent phone conversation with Charlie.

The books were clean. That was Charlie's report. He had gone through them twice and found nothing anomalous, nothing that failed to add up. No missing funds that suddenly disappeared or double accounting to make money look like it was there when it wasn't. He heard the disappointed acceptance in my voice; I was hoping to uncover something and be able to start a search from there. It wasn't to be though until he said, 'The books were last adjusted only a few hours before you sent them to me. I thought that might be important.'

'What do you mean by adjusted?'

'Only that the file had been overwritten and saved just a few hours ago. If I had the authorisation code I could go in and change all the figures now if I wanted to, make the books read completely differently. So, if there was anything anomalous in the historical data, it could have been erased.'

I thought about that for a moment, asking myself what it could mean. 'Would anyone be able to overwrite historical account data?'

'Goodness, no, Patricia,' Charlie chuckled as if I had said something really dumb. 'If we were to let them do that, they could fudge the figures ten ways to Sunday. Only a couple of people would have the authority to do that and then they have to go through a process to record the changes they made.' Basically, only the bursar and probably his deputy would have the ability to overwrite and save the account data so since it had occurred in the hours before Julian's body was found but after the time recorded for his death, the likely killer was suddenly Commander Krill or maybe Lieutenant Commander Singh. We planned to watch both of them tonight.

I hadn't known about the account being overwritten when I decided I wanted to follow people, but the targets hadn't changed. I had a prime suspect now though; the bursar was acting shifty and definitely had the ability to overwrite the pension account details. I wasn't yet ready to point the finger at him – I still had no idea what was going on or why Julian had been killed. Until I figured that out, I couldn't construct a case. So we were also going to follow the deputy bursar, Lieutenant Scott, and Ensign Gosnell for good measure.

Deepa messaged to say Ensign Gosnell was in the crew bar and looked set to be there a while. There was a soccer match he was sitting down to watch with a dozen other fellows, so I wrote him off as far as following people went. I questioned Shannon's likely involvement; she wouldn't have the authority to fiddle with the accounts to hide whatever was there before. However, she might have been lying about the deputy bursar, she was unpopular with the other staff and when she left the ship by herself and looked dolled up for a date, the back of my head started itching again.

A message from Martin helped. 'Lieutenant Commander Singh is on route to the crew exit. I am following.'

I called Deepa. 'Deepa, where are you?'

'Just about to leave the ship. Are you still close by?'

I looked up at the crew exit, a small door just along from the passenger main exit. Barbie raised an arm to identify herself as Deepa came onto the gangplank. She spotted us but I didn't want to hang around.

'Guys, we need to split up. Jermaine and I will follow the bursar, here he comes now. Can you two follow Lieutenant Scott and ask Deepa and Martin to stick with Lieutenant Commander Singh? We don't need to follow them all night. Just long enough to find out where they are going and if they are meeting anyone. Okay?' Everyone nodded so I looped my arm through Jermaine's, and we set off after the bursar as he passed us, with Anna tugging me along in her desperation to get wherever we were going.

With so many people all leaving the ship at one time, it was easy to stay invisible in the crowd. They buoyed us along as we went with the tide, the bursar easy to spot because he wore a rather bright shirt. He paused at one point and we got closer to him than intended. I thought we might have to pass him and then try to loop around rather than also stop and make it obvious that we were on his tail. He appeared to be checking his phone, probably getting his bearings using a map function since he spent half his time staring at it, but he started moving again before we needed to make a decision about our next move.

His pause brought us into close proximity with him, which allowed me to pick up his clean smell and whiff of aftershave. I could smell shampoo, so he had also put in effort for someone tonight. Now I wished I had paid more attention to his file because I was sure I could remember seeing a wedding ring on his hand earlier and that would mean he had a family on board. A wife at the very least.

'Can you see his left hand?' I asked Jermaine.

He dodged his head about a bit, looking for a better view. 'I cannot, madam,' he concluded after a while. I would have to get closer to confirm he was up to what I thought he was up to.

It was twilight in Athens, the streets filled with local people stopping in bars and restaurants on their way home. It made for good cover but also made it more likely we would lose our quarry if we didn't pay attention. I used my phone to send a quick message to Deepa. 'How are you getting on?'

A few seconds later, her answer came back. 'He went into the first restaurant he found and is sitting alone, reading a book, and looking relaxed. I think this is a bust. We are going to get some dinner for ourselves just across the street so we can keep watching.'

I sent back an, 'Okay,' then messaged Barbie with the same question.

Her reply didn't come back immediately though. Ahead of us, the bursar continued to fiddle with his phone, turning it this way and that as if trying to orientate it. I would have the same problem; I knew my phone had a map function but the one time I had tried to use it, I got hopelessly lost and ended up going around in circles in Hawaii. In the end I bought a map from a petrol station I stumbled across, got them to tell me where I was and made my way back the ship. The bursar was looking for something or trying to get somewhere and was unfamiliar with either Athens itself, or just didn't know where the destination was in relationship to his current location.

Jermaine steered me to look at a restaurant menu on a stand in the street while the bursar continued to struggle. A young woman instantly spotted us and tried to guide us inside, promising us the best meal in Athens. Anna liked the sound of that or maybe she just liked the food smells wafting out because she was trying to drag me inside and being encouraged by the waitress who was proving to be persistent. When I failed to go inside, she assured us we would fall in love if we would only come inside and eat. When I gave up being polite and walked away, the bursar was gone. I blushed as I said several rude words.

Finally, Barbie called me. She spoke quietly as she whispered, 'We are at the Hotel Tiare on a street labelled as Artis. Shannon just went inside. It has a restaurant on the ground floor, but she walked past about two hundred restaurants to get here so...'

'She must be there to meet someone,' I finished her sentence. I had a pretty good idea who it was too. 'Stay there. We are coming to you.' I disconnected the call and handed my phone to Jermaine.

'We need to get to the Hotel Tiare on a street called Artis. Barbie said that's where Shannon is, and I think she went there to meet the bursar for an evening of extra-marital activity.'

'Really?' Jermaine questioned. His fingers were doing things with my phone even as he said it. Looking up, he pointed. 'That way, madam. It's not far.'

I tugged at his arm. 'We need to hurry. I want to get there before him.'

'Very good, madam.' He broke into a jog, his long legs delivering powerful strides, forcing me to run, not jog, just to keep up. Why hadn't I worn my running shoes? Mercifully, I had chosen ballet pumps and not heels but they still weren't designed for running in.

Anna, fast despite the short legs, was bounding along and threatening to trip one or both of us.

As I drew level with his shoulder, Jermaine said, 'They seem an ill-matched couple, don't you think?'

I knew what he meant. I had instantly dismissed the notion that they might be romantically involved when it first occurred to me. Stranger relationships occur though and maybe this was about him having power over her career and her influencing his decisions. I hoped to corner them and find out soon enough because a triangle had formed. The bursar was one of the only people that could fiddle with the accounts to overwrite them and he was involved with Shannon, a woman who Julian had expressed an interest in. The bursar could easily use her charms to distract Julian and kill him. They might both be involved in the murder.

As that thought occurred to me, and my breath started to catch on my chest from the effort of running, I spotted the hotel.

Getting it Wrong

As we approached the hotel and the light pouring from it, we slowed our pace to a walk. We hadn't caught up to or passed the bursar but the streets were old and narrow and zigzagged so there were dozens of routes he could have taken, not least because he gave the appearance of being lost.

Hideki stepped out of a shadow on the other side of the street, closely followed by Barbie. 'Did we get here first?' I asked, still trying to catch my breath.

'First?' Hideki questioned.

'Sorry.' I realised I hadn't told them who to expect. 'We were following the bursar, but we lost him. I'm pretty sure he is on his way here to meet Shannon.'

'The bursar?' Barbie questioned, her face screwing up in disgust. 'Stinky Pete?'

Now Hideki stared at her, failing to understand the reference. 'His name is Peter?' he asked.

'It's from a film,' she said dismissively. 'You really think he's been getting it on with Shannon Scott? Why would she do that? I mean... ewwww!'

It was a fair question and one I wouldn't mind knowing the answer to. She wouldn't be the first woman in history to choose a lesser mate for a greater advantage. It would be nice if sex was all about love but none of us were that naïve.

Having beaten him here, all we needed to do now was wait. We didn't need to do that in the street though, we could go inside and take a seat, get a drink and maybe even order some food.

The hotel didn't look like much from the outside, but we discovered it looked worse on the inside. The thought of ordering food from the menu evaporated as soon as we saw that no one else was eating – a sure sign that it was being avoided.

Taking that in, Hideki said, 'Nevermind. They can't mess up bottled beer or wine so I'll get a round in and we can look for somewhere better to eat shortly. This won't take long, will it?' We grabbed a table as he went to the bar, but we finished our drinks twenty minutes later and the bursar still hadn't showed up.

I blew out a sigh of exasperation as I accepted that I had got it wrong. Then I pushed back my chair and stood up, the tension of inactivity filling me with nervous energy. 'Jermaine sweetie, can you distract the chap on reception while I get a look at the ledger, please? I want to see what room Shannon is staying in.'

The chap on reception doubled as the barman so all Jermaine needed to do was go to the bar. The reception desk was still in full view though as Jermaine started asking the man about his wine selection. Barbie and Hideki provided a human wall to disguise my movements while I slipped stealthily behind the reception desk to look at the screen. It was simple enough to navigate but when I glanced across to make sure the barman wasn't watching, I discovered that he was. To take attention away from me, Barbie and Hideki were kissing. Passionately. Everyone in the bar was looking their way and therefore also my way and I was caught with my hand in the proverbial till.

I froze like a rabbit in headlights, brain scrambling to come up with a reason why I was behind the reception desk but I could see from the barman's scowl that he wasn't buying any excuses.

'Time to go,' I yelled at Barbie and Hideki.

The barman, perhaps thinking I was trying to rob the place, grabbed a small wooden club from behind the bar and hefted it as he made his way towards us, shouting and gesturing and most likely throwing Grecian expletives around for all to hear.

Another man appeared, popping his head out of a door behind reception to see what all the ruckus was. I was already moving but he spotted me, saw the barman coming my way and tried to grab my arm. I squealed and darted out of his range. The new man was heavyset and in his late fifties. He could be the owner but whoever he was, he intended to stop me leaving.

Unfortunately for him, I had my miniscule guard dog with me. She snapped at his leg as he advanced, drawing Barbie's attention. Her lips were unlocked from Hideki's now and Anna's bark made her look my way. As the heavyset man made another grab for me, this time trying to get hold of my hair, Hideki struck his forearm, the blow having enough power in it to put the man off. The barman reached the end of the bar but his focus was on us so he didn't see Jermaine deftly put out a foot to trip him. As he sprawled on the carpet, the four us of fled the crappy hotel and I decided tonight's quest was a bust. The only thing we should do now is find somewhere nice to eat and then head back to the ship.

We burst from the hotel doors as a tangled mass and ran the next hundred yards to put some distance between us and anyone that might choose to chase us. No one followed though and as we looked at each other and got our breath back, Barbie sniggered. 'How do we always end up getting into trouble?' she asked. Thus started a fun discussion about the barman's angry face and how our silly ruse hadn't worked at all.

Athens is easy to navigate if one wished to find the port because one needed only to walk downhill. I looked around as we made our way back to the more central business areas, taking in as much as I could as we walked past churches and statues and fountains. It was beautiful, but a lull in the conversation allowed me to hear the groan.

I glanced at Jermaine; he heard it too. My feet stopped moving, which, after a few paces caused Barbie and Hideki to stop walking as well. 'What is it?' she asked, seeing the concern on my face.

I held up a finger for quiet and we all listened. This time the groan sounded like someone calling pitifully for help. The ancient streets were crisscrossed with even narrower alleyways, but when the sound came again, we all pinpointed its direction.

Tucked off the street, in a dark alleyway, lying in a pool of his own blood, was the bursar.

Murder

He was slumped onto his side and clinging to life even as it seeped out of him. His chest was a mess of stab marks, his shirt slashed in several places and blood bubbling out of his chest where at least one of his lungs had been punctured.

Barbie, well versed in emergency first aid as part of her crew training, and Hideki, a final year medical student, set to work on him but I was certain it was already too late.

'I need to call an ambulance,' I blurted, suddenly waking up from the shock of seeing the bursar in such a state. I pulled Anna away, her natural curiosity making her dig in her claws for purchase as she tried to get to the man on the ground. Bringing up the keypad function, I then had to ask, 'What's the number for emergency services in Greece?' I was trying to keep my voice under control, but I was flustered. I was getting used to seeing dead bodies but this one was still alive and might hold the answers to everything if we could just keep him alive until some paramedics arrived.

'Nine one one,' shouted Barbie. 'Just like home. My home that is, not yours.'

I punched in the numbers and got through to a dispatcher somewhere. They answered in Greek of course but I didn't get the chance to identify myself and ask if they spoke English because the cops showed up anyway.

They had their guns drawn and were shouting instructions in their native tongue, neither one seeming to speak English until one said. 'Hands! Hands now! Mother Hubbard!'

'Mother Hubbard?' I felt certain he had gotten wrong what he was trying to say but his intent was clear. I raised my hands. As I did, I noticed a large smear of blood on my right forearm and then the blood that stained the hem of my dress when I stooped to see the bursar and must have dipped it in the pool flowing out from him.

Jermaine heard them shouting and left the dark alleyway to join me, his hands safely raised. He startled them though, a large black man emerging from a dark space. Then Anna barked and the cop nearest him squeezed off a shot in surprise.

I screamed.

Jermaine instinctively went into protection mode and took out both cops in a flurry of arms and legs and then our evening, which hadn't been a triumph, went right downhill.

I wasn't hit by the stray bullet mercifully; it passed by to embed itself in the mortar of the wall behind me. It gave me quite a fright though, my heart racing still when the next wave of cops arrived a few seconds later. The first pair had probably radioed for backup when they first saw me covered in blood but the gunshot doubled their pace so they too arrived with their guns drawn. Jermaine and I kept our hands up and did our best to look harmless despite the blood on my skin and clothing and the two disarmed cops rolling on the ground.

'Everyone okay out there?' asked Barbie's disembodied voice from the dark alleyway. The two new cops were calmer than their colleagues, one radioing for yet more backup while the other gave simple gesticulations for us to get on the ground augmented by speaking in broken English.

Jermaine and I did as we were told, getting on our knees and keeping our hands visible. Over the top of the policeman's instructions, I called to Barbie. 'How's he doing?'

She didn't answer for a moment but when she did, a small sob came with it. 'He's gone.'

Someone had killed him. Stabbed him multiple times in a frenzied attack and left him to bleed to death. Was it the same killer? If so, what had Julian uncovered? The two murders were too close together and too interlinked by their jobs for me to easily believe this was a coincidence. However, they were so different. The first was well-thought out and carefully executed. In fact, had the killer not written the suicide note and used Julian's left hand for the gun I would most likely have not questioned it. This though; this was passionate or angry. An attack fuelled by rage perhaps. Could a killer go from one to the other?

I didn't know the answer but as the cuffs closed over my wrists, I was certain I wasn't going to get anything productive done tonight.

A Night in a Cell

A female officer at the station spoke fluent English which at least meant we were able to protest our innocence and have them understand what we were saying. Despite that they took Anna away, which I really wasn't happy about. Animal services would hold her, the female officer said; they didn't have the facility to manage animals at the station. The duty sergeant listened to her translate my complaints, but he wasn't interested in doing anything beyond processing us and getting us into cells. He told us an English-speaking lawyer had been requested, we could each have one phone call in due course, and we should do our best to make ourselves comfortable. If we were innocent, we had nothing to worry about.

I for one didn't find his reassurance very reassuring.

They let us clean the blood from our skin but only once they took a stack of photographs. We had to wait for the phone call though and I wasn't sure who to call. The obvious person would be Alistair at any other time than the day his nephew was found dead. He was having dinner with the mayor of Athens and several other local dignitaries this evening which meant he had exactly the right people with him if I wanted to get out of here quickly. Thankfully, I didn't have to make that call because Jermaine did it for me, making contact with the ship to alert them to our… situation. Word would reach Alistair soon enough.

I figured the cops had arrested us out of confusion because there was a body and we were all covered in blood from it. Add to that, the fact that Jermaine disarmed two of the cops when one nearly shot me, and it was hardly surprising we were now incarcerated while they sorted out the mess.

I lay back on the narrow, hard bunk with its wafer-thin mattress and ran through some scenarios in my head. I guess I didn't do it for long though because the next thing I knew, I was being woken up by the cell door opening. I had lost track of the number of times I had been locked up recently, even smirking to myself that I was touring the world by visiting all of its jails.

It was a cop opening my cell this time though, not one of my friends performing an elaborate jail break. A man in a good suit came in with his hand out to greet me. 'Good evening, I'm Manos Katrakis your court appointed lawyer. I don't think this will take very long. Your captain just arrived with the mayor and the chief of police. The mayor is making quite a fuss at the front desk. It seems they didn't recognise you, Mrs Fisher. The saviour of Zangrabar, isn't that what they call you?'

I nodded my head, feeling the weight of that particular title hanging heavy around my neck. Everyone but me felt that I deserved it. Maybe it was going to help me out a little here though.

The sound of Alistair's raised voice reached my ears. I couldn't quite make out what he was saying but he was letting someone have it. The lawyer peered out through the tiny eye-height panel in the cell door, watching and clearly expecting to be let out again soon.

'They bungled, you see,' he announced suddenly. It made me feel as if I had woken up halfway through a conversation. 'The firearm being discharged in the street really goes against them. Ah, here they are,' he smiled over his shoulder as someone approached down the corridor outside. 'I suspect the chief of police made it simple for them. They already admitted they found no murder weapon and it was clear you were trying to help the poor man.'

The cell door opened but the cop had already moved on to the next cell where he was letting Jermaine out. Soon all four of us were being led back through to the station's main reception desk where I could spot several white uniforms; Alistair came in force.

Deprived of my phone and watch, I had lost track of time and was surprised to see the clock on the wall said it was almost three in the morning. Alistair beckoned for me to join him as our belongings were brought out to us. I'm sure it wasn't the usual way things were done but I was still missing one very important accessory. 'Where's Anna?' I asked.

'Animal services are taking her to the ship,' Alistair assured me. 'Let's just get you back there too, shall we. It's been a long day.' I was glad of his help, his presence felt reassuring and soon I started to fall asleep again in the back of the cruise line's limousine. As my eyes snapped open despite the lead weights forcing them closed, I considered my day and what I had achieved with it. The answer was not very much. I was no closer to working out who killed Julian or why and now I had a second murder to consider.

I asked Alistair about it. What he told me was, 'They said it was most likely a mugging gone wrong. His wallet and watch were stolen. Their guess was that he decided to fight the mugger and got killed for his efforts.'

I didn't believe it, but if I were the killer and had deliberately targeted the bursar, would I have left him to bleed out in the street when it would be so easy to finish him off and be sure he couldn't identify me? It felt clumsy compared to the first murder. So maybe it was a mugging gone wrong. After all, he had wandered far out of the tourist areas and into a seedy part of the city.

I sat bolt upright in my seat making Alistair jump. 'Good grief, Patricia, what is it?'

The great ship filled the windscreen now; we were on the quayside and about to stop. A small van with a picture of a dog behind bars on the back was pulled up next to the main passenger entrance and a man in a set of brown overalls was trying to hand over Anna to the pair of security guards there.

I needed to check on something and it wasn't going to wait until daybreak. 'We need to go back into Athens,' I blurted at Alistair as I grabbed my door handle. The moment the car stopped I jumped out and whistled for my dog.

She barked instantly and began struggling for the man to put her down. He juggled her a bit, but probably on orders to give the dog back, something I doubted animal control did very often, he got her to the tarmac and let her go. 'Come to mummy, sweetie.' My call of encouragement was one hundred percent unnecessary because she was already heading my way as fast as she could go.

'Why are we going back?' asked Alistair.

I scooped Anna and fell back into the car. 'We need to get to Hotel Tiare on Artis Street right now. We probably want some back up as well because they won't be pleased to see me.'

Alistair stared into my eyes for a second, then said to the driver, 'You heard the lady.'

Extra-Marital Affairs

Alistair sent a squad of armed security guards into the hotel in front of us. Their weapons were securely holstered but the effect was about the same. When I strolled in, being led by Anna a minute later, the barman from earlier had been roused from his bed and was staring open mouthed and bleary eyed at the white uniformed force now occupying reception.

He stared at me, clearly recognising me, but kept his mouth shut; a wise move given the circumstances. When one of the security team stepped forward and started to speak to him in fluent Greek, his attention shifted from my face to his.

'One good thing about having a ship full of crew from every corner of the globe,' observed Alistair quietly, 'you can always find someone that speaks the local language.'

The conversation between the guard and the barman was short, resulting in the guard turning around to report, 'Room fourteen on the first floor, sir.'

'We need a key,' I pointed out. A brief exchange of words later and the barman handed over a large silver thing attached to an even bigger lump of brass.

This didn't require all of us but everyone went upstairs anyway, the noise of so many boots on wooden stairs surely sufficient to wake anyone asleep in the hotel. I carried Anna up the stairs and popped her back on the creaking floorboards right outside room number fourteen.

The moment of truth.

Alistair turned the key and opened the door, the action waking the person inside. It was just one person, exactly as I expected. Terrified because people were entering her room uninvited in the night, she grabbed the first thing her hand came to, which just happened to be a shoe, and she launched it at the door, screaming obscenities in her fright.

Alistair flicked on the light and I prayed she had some clothes on or the covers pulled up. Her hand was reaching for something else to throw but the sight of two people she recognised gave her pause. 'Captain?' Quietly, Alistair closed the door behind us, shutting out the faces of several members of the security team who were peering around the doorframe to see if the statuesque blonde was naked.

Keeping his eyes down because Shannon was clearly naked beneath her bedsheets, Alistair said, 'I apologise for the intrusion, Lieutenant Scott.' She was angry. Too angry to care about holding her tongue and why should she? Shore leave was private time for the crew and the captain had no right to interrupt it.

Nevertheless, before she could say something she might regret, I said something that stopped her cold. 'William Krill isn't coming Shannon.'

She started to shake her head in denial but sensing the pointlessness of such an action, she just said, 'I figured that out for myself when he didn't show.'

'You do know he was married, don't you?' Alistair pointed out; his disapproval obvious.

She had a snappy comeback ready to fire but it died on her lips. 'Was... You said was. Has something happened to him?'

Softly, Alistair told her about the mugging. He told her how he was on his way to her when the attack occurred and how I had tried to save him. I wanted to leave. I needed to come here to prove a theory to myself, but now that task was complete, there was no reason for me to remain and every reason for me to leave. Suddenly unable to stand her sadness any longer, I blurted that I had to go and let myself out. The security team were still in the corridor, quietly waiting for their captain to finish. Lieutenant Scott had broken a rule in not disclosing the relationship but couldn't have done that without breaking another rule as she was involved with a married man whose wife was on board the ship. Either way, she would be dismissed so had lost her lover and her livelihood in one night.

What had I learned? The bursar had been conducting an affair that would have severely damaged his career and most likely curtailed any future prospect of promotion. Was that what had him so jittery during our interview? I felt at the time that he was trying to hide something. I thought it would be something bigger but perhaps it was just an illicit relationship. I couldn't ask him now, but I doubted he had killed Julian because he found out and threatened to expose them. That just seemed too far-fetched and if it hadn't been the case, then who killed the bursar?

I was tired. That much I was certain of and no one's brain works well when it is fatigued so I let the problem go. For more than twenty hours, I had been pursuing the truth about Julian Young's death. My results were spectacularly poor.

I fell asleep on the ride back to the ship and fell into my bed after Alistair dropped me off in my suite. He didn't stay and I didn't ask him to. However badly my day had gone, his had been far harder to endure.

Tomorrow I would start again.

Breakfast Hit and Miss

The Aurelia was due to leave Athens at 1300hrs, the visit to Greece one of the shortest stops on the entire trip. I was disappointed by how little of it I had seen – so far as I was concerned, the police station didn't count as a tourist attraction. Despite being tired, I forced myself out of bed and into the shower. I intended to do more digging today, to see if I could make more headway than I had in the previous twenty-four hours, but Athens beckoned and I was going to see it in the daylight whether it was practical to do so or not.

Coming out of my bedroom, I discovered Deepa Bhukari and Martin Baker already waiting for me. They each had a steaming mug of coffee and Anna wedged between them where they had chosen to both sit on one couch.

I got, 'Good morning, Mrs Fisher,' from both and replied in kind. They were dressed in their uniforms and ready to get back to the investigation. I needed to get my engine started before I could consider that though.

Jermaine handed me my own mug of coffee. 'Good morning, madam. I trust you slept well.'

I sipped the dark brew. 'Very well, thank you.' Turning so I could address the room, I announced, 'I'm going ashore for breakfast. I didn't see anything of Athens yesterday. Who wants to join me?' When no one responded immediately, I added, 'My treat.'

For me, one of the things about going all the way around the planet was getting to try all the different cuisines. I had no idea what they ate for breakfast in Greece, but I was going to find out. As if sensing my intention to leave, Anna plopped off the couch and began to stretch, pushing her front legs forward to ease off her shoulders and then pushing her back legs back. Somehow she made herself twice as long.

I got dressed quickly, gulping down the strong coffee and feeling its rejuvenating powers as the caffeine hit my veins. Twenty minutes after falling out of bed, I was ready to go. Certain in my head that my days ashore shouldn't have to be this rushed, I nevertheless felt serious pressure to get back to the investigation. There was a killer somewhere among us, that much I knew, and that fact alone made leaving the ship to get breakfast and have a nose around feel like an unnecessary indulgence.

So I told myself that Anna needed a walk and combining the tasks of walkies and breakfast was an efficiency. Whatever the case, we soon found a delightful looking eatery overlooking the quayside and the beautiful bay beyond. The young lady who brought us menus must have thought I was a famous film star or perhaps a billionaire when I arrived with my own butler and what appeared to be a two-person security team. It only threw her for a moment though, pausing while Jermaine pushed in my chair and then handing out menus.

I had chosen to wear big sunglasses and a wide-brimmed hat this morning. They went with my summer dress nicely but more than that, they disguised my face which all too many people recognised now after it circled the globe on the front of every newspaper. There had been requests for interviews, many of which came with the offer of a payment. I turned them all down. Why would anyone be interested to hear what I had to say? To me, it seemed more likely I would embarrass myself even further and a deep-rooted mistrust of the press, where I got it from I could not say, whispered that they would ask me daft questions about my choice of underwear instead of anything worthwhile.

The young waitress returned a few minutes later to take our order. I was already in need of more coffee, my total hours of sleep last night having been somewhere between four and five, but when I started to place my order, I spotted someone.

'Madam,' prompted Jermaine.

'Hmm?'

'Madam, your order for breakfast.' I squinted into the distance, decided I was right and got to my feet. Anna bounced back onto her feet too, ready to go wherever it was we were going.

My companions looked bewildered for a moment, but then, perhaps remembering that it was me and I am a little eccentric, they followed my gaze and saw what I was staring at.

'That's Ensign Gosnell,' said Deepa Bhukari looking at her watch. It was early to have been out already, have performed whatever task had driven him from the ship and be returning.

I asked anyway, 'Do you think he went out for breakfast as well?'

She pulled a face as she mulled the idea over. 'He's still wearing his clothes from last night.' She tutted. 'I thought he was staying in the bar. That's why I didn't follow him. He looked set to be there all evening.'

Lieutenant Baker started for the street. 'Well, let's find out where he went.' I had to weave around the table, made more difficult by Anna tugging to follow Baker's departing feet. Ensign Gosnell had been in my initial pool of suspects. The report of his behaviour when his account went to Julian was suspicious, but little more than that, and I dismissed him when he failed to do anything interesting last night. Now I questioned that decision.

'Ensign Gosnell,' called Lieutenant Baker, making sure his voice was loud enough to carry to the other man's ears. His head whipped around to see where the shout came from, so we all saw his eyes widen and the look of panic on his face. I hadn't expected him to run though.

Lieutenant Baker, who was a few yards ahead of us, looked back at us with an expression that said, 'What the heck?' then started jogging after our quarry. Ensign Gosnell was doing his best impression of an Olympic sprinter, tearing along the street back toward the Aurelia, but he wasn't in complete control of his body. As I watched, he bounced off a couple when he meant to go around them, and then staggered as he tried to get up. He looked drunk. He was running though, trying to get away which was pointless since he was clearly heading for the Aurelia, which is where we found him a few minutes later.

Deepa radioed ahead the moment we left the restaurant, alerting the security guards at the ship's entrance and arranging for the panicked ensign to be held there. We could hear him arguing with them as we approached.

I heard him insist, 'I need to get back to my cabin.'

But his protestations had little impact on the security guard. 'You'll wait where you are Ensign Gosnell. Someone wishes to speak with you.'

The four of us, led by Anna and still devoid of breakfast, walked up the gangplank and in through the crew entrance. Lieutenant Baker got to him first. 'Why did you run?'

'I thought you were someone else?' he replied, his nervousness clear. Baker looked down at himself. He wore immaculate, bright white shorts and a short-sleeved shirt, knee-high white socks rolled down to the top of his black boots. He had a white hat with a black peak and a black utility belt with a holstered gun: who else could he look like?

Baker didn't respond to his comment though. He turned to his colleague Deepa Bhukari saying, 'We need an interview room.'

Guilty of Something

As we stood in the shade just inside the crew entrance, the first thing I noticed was the blood on Ensign Gosnell's shirt. There was a splatter of it across the front and more drops on his trousers. His expression was guilty, but what was he guilty of? Keeping my lips firmly pressed closed to prevent questions tumbling from them, I followed Baker and Bhukari through the ship.

At an elevator, Baker put a hand out to stop me following any further. 'We need to process him, take his personal effects, bag his clothing so we can test the blood on it. All of that will take time. You might as well take the opportunity to get some breakfast, Mrs Fisher.' I nodded as I accepted my questions would have to wait. Ensign Gosnell had killed the bursar last night and I was desperate to find out why. I had missed something, that was what I was telling myself, beating myself up for my lack of intuition.

'Will you call for me when you are ready?'

'Of course, Mrs Fisher. The captain made it clear we were to include you in every part of this investigation.' I worried my inclusion might be perceived as an insult to the security team. It was their job to solve this crime, not mine. I was only thrown into the mix because Alistair thought I might help but they acted as if they were pleased to have me along. I thanked Lieutenant Baker and promised to be ready, my stomach announcing its emptiness with a loud growl while we were speaking as if to accentuate the need for me to put something in it.

I turned to Jermaine as the elevator doors closed. 'What is your desire, madam?' We had a little time to kill but I wasn't going ashore again; that all just felt like too much effort for too little reward. Most likely, I would be annoyed that I could see Athens stretching out before me and had no time to explore it. 'Perhaps just some fruit and toast?' I asked.

With a small dip of his head, he said, 'Very good, madam. On the sun terrace this morning? The elevated position will give an excellent view over the city.' He was doing his best to make up for missing Athens; he knew how much I had been looking forward to exploring.

'Thank you, Jermaine. That would be perfect.' And it was. I couldn't get into the city but there was nothing to be gained by crying about it. I could always come back one day, the flight from England couldn't be more than three or four hours. Instead, for now, I watched the city, listened to its sounds and thought about Julian Young.

It wasn't really a conscious decision to consider him. However, with

Ensign Gosnell in custody downstairs and the unshakeable belief that he murdered Commander Krill last night, the connection between the case and the two homicides was inescapable. That the young ensign had killed his superior was in no doubt so far as I was concerned but I needed to work out why. Without understanding why, unless Gosnell gave a confession, I was going to struggle to prove he also killed Julian.

I found myself getting antsy waiting for Lieutenant Baker to call me, so when my phone rang, I snatched it up. 'Are you ready?' I asked without preamble.

'Ready for what, sweetie?' asked a familiar voice.

My brain took a second to catch up. 'Lady Mary?'

'Yes, sweetie. What time is it there? Because it's gin o'clock here!' she announced with a cheeky laugh.

'Lady Mary, it's so nice to hear your voice.' I realised then that I missed my friend. We didn't get to spend much time together, little more than a week, but had hit it off very quickly and then found ourselves in a situation that gave us shared memories and a closeness we might never lose. With Rick and Akamu gone, I felt a little alone; there was no one my age in my circle unless one included Alistair.

'Well, Patricia dear, I'm surprised you could find the time to answer. You're quite the celebrity now.'

I smiled ironically to myself. 'Yes. I'm certainly something. Is this a social call?'

There was a pause followed by a glugging noise. 'Sorry, sweetie, the contents of my glass appear to have evaporated.' I wondered if she was on her second, third or twelfth. It was noon at home in England and I knew she liked to start at breakfast. I had to wait for her to finish making her drink, getting a running commentary as she loaded cracked ice, not cubes, then garnished the drink with a slice of cucumber and tested it for consistency and strength. She could host a late-night television show where she got the home audience drunk getting them to copy her cocktails. Finally ready to tell me why she called, she said, around a swig of gin, 'I'm coming back to the ship, sweetie.'

I was surprised to find myself quite excited at the prospect of seeing her again. When she left, we promised to find each other when my cruise finished. Now I didn't have to wait that long. 'When?' I gushed.

'I'm flying out tomorrow. I'll meet you in Malta. George is on another of his silly book tours. I honestly don't know why he bothers; the books sell themselves, but I think he likes the adulation from his fans.'

'How long are you staying on board?'

'All the way back to Southampton, sweetie.' This was such great news. I loved Jermaine and Barbie and the others I got to spend time with regularly, but I was a mature woman now and often craved company with which I had more in common.

We talked for a few minutes, catching up on each other's lives. She asked me about Zangrabar and if any other exciting events had interrupted my peaceful cruise. I laughed out loud at her question and promised to fill her in properly when I saw her in Malta; there was too much to list now. To give her something, I revealed my relationship with the captain and could hear the masked jealousy in her voice though I knew she didn't really want to replace her husband; George was very sweet even if he was a bit doughy and bald now.

Chatting away, my phone beeped in my ear, signalling another call coming in. Looking at the screen, I could see Lieutenant Bhukari's number displayed. Lady Mary's call had caused the imminent interview with Ensign Gosnell to slip my mind.

'I have to go, Mary. Let me know when you are arriving on the boat. I'll have the gin chilled and ready.'

'You make sure you do that, sweetie.'

Then she was gone, and I could answer the other call. 'Are you ready?' They were. Ensign Gosnell was cooperating, but he wasn't telling them anything.

They took his personal belongings and had them laid out and labelled for me to inspect when I arrived. He was tucked away in a room somewhere to stew.

It took me a while to get there again, going from the top deck almost to the bottom. I looked through his personal effects: wallet, loose change, his phone. The wallet was full of local currency. So much of it that it was a struggle to close it. 'Did he say where the money came from?' I asked the tall member of the security team behind the desk in the brig.

'Claimed he won it gambling, Mrs Fisher.' If it was a lie, it was a good one – how could we prove otherwise?'

'Where's the clothing?' Determining if the blood belonged to Commander Krill was a priority. If Gosnell wouldn't talk but we found the commander's blood on his shirt, it would place him directly at the scene. He didn't need to confess to be proven guilty. The murder occurred on Greek soil so we would probably have to turn him over for trial in Greece if he was guilty – I wasn't sure of the legalities of it since Commander Krill was Russian and not Greek. It was a consideration for later though.

The absent clothing was already with Dr Kim who claimed to be able to match the blood closely enough from a tiny swabbed sample. Deepa told me they sent someone to my suite to collect my dress from last night since the blood on that was Commander Krill's, and that was what he would match Ensign Gosnell's stains to. If it was the same as the sample taken from my dress, he would be able to show it and then a proper crime lab would be able to perform more reliable tests that could be used in court.

I called him to see how long that would take. 'Dr Kim, good morning...'

'Mrs Fisher,' he interrupted me talking fast. 'You are calling about the blood matching test I offered to perform. I'm afraid that has been forced to take a back seat. I have a badly injured crew member in my care. It looks like he took quite the beating last night. I'll call you back.' He hung up. Rudeness was not his norm, though I forgave him; he sounded flustered and busy.

There being nothing else to delay us, I followed Baker and Bhukari to the interview room. The door was guarded by another member of the security team, a tall man who stepped aside to let us go inside before resuming his position.

Baker began with some formalities. 'Ensign Gosnell you have waived the right to have a senior member of the ship's crew present, please confirm that for the recorder.'

'That is correct,' he replied, his voice croaking with his nerves.

'For the recording equipment, this interview is being conducted by

Lieutenant Martin Baker and Lieutenant Deepa Bhukari, both members of the Aurelia security detail. Mrs Patricia Fisher is observing as a special consultant.'

I was observing. What I could see was how guilty Ensign Gosnell looked. His eyes were darting about, lingering for no time at all in every place they landed: me, Baker, the clock on the wall, the door, his hands, back to me. That he was guilty of something was obvious and I was fairly certain he had killed the bursar in a brutal knife attack last night.

I just needed to figure out why and if it was connected to Julian's death.

Lieutenant Baker started the interview, having Ensign Gosnell state his name and a few other details and then got into asking where he had been, why he ran when Baker called his name, where the blood on his clothing came from. Ensign Gosnell refused to answer any questions. He kept saying he had done nothing wrong and didn't know why we were holding him. He didn't deny that there was blood on his shirt but instead of saying he didn't know how it got there, he refused to give an answer at all.

Baker did his best to keep his frustration in check. He might have to wear Ensign Gosnell down and to do so he needed to be patient and in control. Deepa Bhukari took over after a while, asking many of the same questions but in a different way. She saw him settling down to watch a soccer match the previous evening, how was it he came to stay out all night and return the next day with blood on his clothes? In asking that question she asserted that he had stayed out all night, but again he refused to answer her question, giving nothing away in the process.

A knock at the door interrupted us. 'Interview paused at 1152hrs.' Baker stabbed the button to stop the disc and pushed back his chair. In over two hours I hadn't said a word. I was working up to it though, working the problem in my head and trying to make the different parts fit. The challenge I faced was that I still didn't have sight of all the parts, and I couldn't see how much of the puzzle was missing.

The knock at the door turned out to be Lieutenant Schneider. Once we were outside with the door locked again, I asked a question. 'Any idea what the mark on his hand is?' I asked assuming the others had seen it.

Deepa Bhukari shook her head. 'Not yet. I sent a picture of it to the local police. Gosnell wouldn't tell us, he said it was nothing, but it looks like the kind of ultra-violet stamp you get at a club. It might be nothing, though it is probably where he went last night after he left the ship.'

As Bhukari fell silent, Schneider started talking. 'I grilled the barman in the crew bar; he was happy enough to provide a full list of everyone in attendance for last night's big match. Some of them had quite a skin full because they had no duties this morning, which made them very ready to answer my questions just to make me go away.'

'Ensign Gosnell left after one drink, didn't he?'

Schneider looked at me. 'Yes, Mrs Fisher. That he did. According to his friends, he was acting weird and jittery. One of them said, "It was like he had taken something." I guess he meant Gosnell couldn't keep still but they also said he spotted you watching him.' He jabbed a finger at Bhukari.

'Dammit,' she swore. 'I interviewed him just a few hours before. He seemed nervous then. He must have seen me watching, waited for me to leave and then snuck out behind me. What on earth has that little creep been up to? Do you think it would be alright for me to beat some answers out of him?'

I knew she was joking but it was a tempting solution. I offered a different option. 'We're getting nowhere, and I don't think Gosnell is going to talk any time soon. Why don't we leave him to stew for a little longer and pester Dr Kim into checking the blood samples?'

Everyone nodded.

Schneider started to lead the way. 'I need to go to the infirmary anyway. One of the chefs got beaten up in town last night and I need to get a statement from him.'

'Any idea what happened?' asked Deepa.

'None so far. He stumbled back to the ship a little after midnight being held up by another man. Jenson and Wong were on the gate, they called for medical assistance but he waved it off, saying he was fine and just needed to get some rest.'

'A drunken brawl then,' concluded Baker.

'That's what I thought but Jenson was adamant that both men were sober. No smell of alcohol on him. He just looked like he had been in a wrestling match with a bear. That's the words they used: wrestling with a bear.'

The Case of the Sasquatch with the Bruised Knuckles

We were quiet most of the rest of the way to the infirmary. Coming from the brig, we needed to go up two decks to get there. We found Dr Kim sitting at his computer writing up notes on a report. As we entered, he was taking a mouthful of coffee, the steam from it fogging up his glasses so when he looked our way, he had to take them off to see who it was.

'Good... afternoon, Dr Kim,' said Lieutenant Schneider, checking his watch as he spoke to confirm the morning had already escaped us. As he said it, I heard the engines rumble into life. The Aurelia was due to slip from its mooring point in under an hour.

Dr Kim waved a quick hello as he placed his glasses back on his face. 'That's better. What can I do for you? Oh! The blood. I completely forgot. I got called to deal with a suspected concussion but then found the patient had three broken ribs, an impacted eye socket, probable internal bleeding and a whole stack of bruises and cuts.'

'Wow!' said Lieutenant Baker. 'Someone really went to town on this guy.'

'More than one person I should think,' replied the doctor.

Curious about his comment, I asked. 'Why is that?'

Dr Kim didn't answer straight away. Instead he got to his feet and went back into the infirmary, passing beds until he got to one with the curtain drawn around it. 'I gave him a sedative because he insisted he was leaving. His concussion isn't life threatening though he could do with an MRI to be certain. However, anyone could see it wasn't his only injury and I wanted to give him a proper examination.'

There was movement behind the curtain which turned out to be a nurse applying dressings. She moved to the side as Dr Kim led us in and I understood why he thought it had to be multiple assailants: the man on the bed was huge.

'Wow!' said Lieutenant Baker for the second time in the last minute. 'It looks like someone shaved a sasquatch.'

'You said he is a chef?'
questioned Lieutenant Bhukari, staring incredulously at the giant on the bed. He chose that moment to shift slightly in his drug-induced slumber, farting loudly as he did. I, for one, didn't hang around any longer and everyone including the nurse elected to give him some privacy as we hurried back to Dr Kim's computer.

'I came to get a statement from him,' huffed Schneider. 'How long do you think he will be out?'

'A few hours unless I give him something to bring him around. The best thing for him now is sleep. Everything will heal but he won't be using his hands to chop anything for a while.'

Once again I found myself confused by Dr Kim's comment. 'Why is that?'

He looked my way. 'Did you not see his hands?'

'No.' I glanced at the curtains, thinking I should go back and have another look but wondered how long I would need to hold my breath and how potent a sasquatch fart might be.

Dr Kim saw my indecision and laughed. 'I have photographs right here.' He pulled the pictures onto his screen, pointing to the knuckles with the end of a pen.

'This sort of injury is usually associated with boxers or with punching something repeatedly. For there to be this amount of damage to his hands, he must have given as good as he got. And judging by the slabs of muscle he calls shoulders, I would expect there to be a few of his attackers in the hospital today.'

It almost felt like there was another mystery to solve: the case of the sasquatch with the bruised knuckles. I shook my head to dismiss the notion and bring myself back to the present. 'The blood, Dr Kim?'

'Oh, yes. I'll get right on that. You can wait if you like. This won't take long.'

A sound from behind me caused my head to swing around, whereupon I saw

Alistair coming through the infirmary door. Schneider, Bhukari and Baker all snapped out crisp salutes and bade him a good day.

Alistair returned the salute. 'Hello, everyone, Patricia, Dr Kim. I understand I have an injured crew member. The ship's company is not having a good run lately.' He wasn't exaggerating; the bursary was already down two personnel including the man in charge and would not get Shannon Scott back in a working capacity due to her illicit and ill-thought affair with Commander Krill. Now Ensign Gosnell was in custody. It was only a matter of time before he was charged with something; quite possibly a double murder.

Before Dr Kim could reply, all four radios squawked. 'Tombola, tombola, tombola. All security report to the helicopter platform immediately.'

Tombola? What the heck did tombola mean? I recognised the nature of the message to be a code word intended to tell the crew a particular event had transpired without blurting any details over the airwaves. Tombola was a new one for me.

In the time it had taken me to question what it might mean in my head, the four crew in white uniform were all running out the door.

'Hey! What does tombola mean?' I shouted as I ran after them.

TOMBOLA

I really had to get my feet moving to catch up with them and would have lost them completely if the elevator had been waiting for them. Out of breath and with a stitch tugging at my side, I tried again. 'What does tombola mean?'

The elevator pinged and we tumbled inside, the captain jabbing the button to get going. Through gritted and impatient teeth, he said, 'It means someone just jumped onto the ship.'

I thought about that and shrugged. 'That doesn't sound too scary. Maybe it's a passenger that missed the loading and managed to jump from the quayside.'

'We put to sea ten minutes ago. It shouldn't be possible to get on the ship.' Alistair looked genuinely worried. 'With everything else that has happened recently, I have to act as if the intruder means harm until we can catch them and prove otherwise.'

We were in a crew elevator that only serviced the bottom seven decks. When it spat us out at the very bottom passenger deck, we then raced to the next elevator to get ourselves to the top of the ship. The captain had an override key on a chain in his pocket which prevented the elevator from stopping at any other decks on its way up. This made the ascent swift; no more than a few seconds to reach the top but then we still had to get to the helicopter pad.

Arriving truly out of breath from trying to keep up with the very fit captain and three members of the security team who each had most of three decades on me, I leaned against the railing to recover as Alistair demanded a report from the team waiting there.

How the person got onto the ship was instantly obvious; a parachute was caught in the railings at the far end of the platform where the wind buffeted and hassled it. I could overhear their conversation, thankfully, so I didn't move, choosing instead to make it look like I was stretching and limbering up after our little race rather than wondering if I was going to vomit over the side onto the passengers on the sun terrace below.

'We saw him in the air, sir. He looked just like any other parasailer; there's lots of them along the coastline. It was only when he turned toward the ship that we looked for the motorboat he should be tethered to and realised there wasn't one.'

'He landed on the helipad?' Alistair confirmed.

'Yes, sir. He went over the side as we got up there though, releasing his paraglider into the breeze so it hit us. By the time we got to the edge, there was no sign of him.'

Alistair pursed his lips in annoyance but patted the man on his shoulder. 'Well done, Silvian. Good reactions. We need to find him now though. You're quite certain the target is a man?'

'Yes, sir. I only caught a glimpse as he went over the rail, but he was wearing a black dinner jacket and trousers like he had just left a casino. He looked at me and tipped a quick salute then was gone.'

Alistair's brow creased in disbelief. 'He gave you a salute?'

'Yes, sir.' The man then gave a quick demonstration, adding a wink as he touched two fingers to his temple. 'Just like that, it was, sir.'

'Riiiight,' drawled the captain. 'Either way, we need to catch him. I don't like unknown guests on my ship. Schneider!'

Lieutenant Schneider jumped to attention. 'Yes, sir?'

'Get some men, rouse Commander Pace and track down that man.'

The guard we found on the helipad wasn't finished though. 'There's something else, sir,'

'Spit it out, man.'

'He's injured, sir. There's blood on the deck and on the railing where he went over.' He led us across to see it for ourselves. It was bright red, which I knew from terrible experience meant it was fresh and from a bad wound.

Alistair knew it too. 'Alright then. You have your blood trail, Lieutenant Schneider. Go catch me an intruder.' Schneider raced away, taking everyone else with him. It left just the captain and me to make our way slowly back down to the upper deck. He offered me his arm as we descended the stairs in the open air. 'Sorry to have stolen away your team. This has to take priority,' he explained.

I waved his apology away. 'I am sure they will not be long with a blood trail to follow. They're looking for a man in a dinner jacket among a crowd of people wearing shorts, vests, and bikinis. I doubt he will be hard to find. Besides, I need time to think.' He had other duties requiring his attention and a manhunt to coordinate so we kissed lightly and I watched him depart on his way back into the ship's superstructure.

Shortly, I would go back to my suite and call Dr Kim. It was lunchtime according to my belly so I would return to the Ensign Gosnell investigation once I had taken a break and walked my dog.

I didn't put any thought to the intruder with the parachute. I probably should have.

Lipreading Dog

Lieutenant Baker had confiscated my universal keycard a short while ago. He was polite about it but insistent. Even though I was using for it for good, he couldn't allow me to hang on to it. I smiled when I handed it over and made a plan to get another one as soon as I could. I hadn't got around to it yet, but it felt like time now – after lunch I wanted to have a poke around Ensign Gosnell's cabin.

Jermaine was in my living area when I returned to my suite. An apron draped from his waist as he dusted using a feather duster. 'Good afternoon, madam.'

'Hello, Jermaine.' He stopped what he was doing to wait for my instructions. My attention went to Anna though as she decided to get off the couch and greet me, her tail wagging excitedly as she waddled across the floor. Waddling was an exaggeration but her tiny nipped-in waist now looked like she had broken into her kibble and gorged herself on it.

I picked her up for a cuddle and carried her through the suite with Jermaine following. 'Might I fix you a beverage, madam?'

I wrestled with the idea for about three seconds before succumbing to temptation. 'Oh, go on then.' I think

Lady Mary's talk of gin caused it to stick in my head as I considered what hour would be acceptable for my first glass several times this morning. Jermaine also prepared a smoked trout salad with pine nuts and clementines. It looked and tasted very healthy so was going to naturally balance out the calories in my drink. That was the lie I told myself, anyway.

Sitting at the breakfast bar in the kitchen rather than at the dining table or on the sun terrace, which I generally avoided when eating because the breeze played havoc with my food, I could feel Anna staring at me.

'What is it, girl?' I asked.

Jermaine looked across at me from the sink where he was washing up. 'She has been pestering me for food as well, madam.'

When I made eye contact with her, she danced about on the spot a bit and chopsed her mouth at me with an accompanying growl intended to get me to do something. She wanted food, that much was obvious, and it suddenly occurred to me that she was most likely eating not just for two, but for five or six now. I wasn't sure how many puppies a Dachshund usually had.

Just about to ask her if she wanted a biscuit, I stopped myself. Anna was staring up at me from the floor, her focus entirely on my face and what I might say next. She didn't understand the words I said though. Like Julian in many ways, she was lipreading. Okay, I didn't think she was lipreading at all, I figured a dog was able to pick up on certain words like dinner or biscuit or walkies and associate them with actions or activities because they get repeated so regularly. The principle was the same though and that got me to thinking about lipreading itself. Absentmindedly, I crossed the kitchen to the bowl of gravy bones and gave her two. I had just glimpsed an answer but it evaded me as soon as I tried to examine it like catching sight of a fish while snorkelling; its scales catch the sun but as soon as you look it has darted away. Focusing made no difference, I couldn't perceive what my brain wanted to tell me, but it was something to do with the case and specifically to do with Julian.

'I'm going to take Anna with me,' I told Jermaine, standing up still lost in my own thoughts. Lunch was done and I still had a mystery to solve. We were at sea now, on our way to Malta where we would arrive in a little less than twenty-four hours.

Anna trotted after me, happy to be getting out of the suite but I was so absorbed by my side-tracked mind that I was at the elevators before I noticed Jermaine came with me too. Even then, I thanked the person for reaching past me to press the call button before I realised it was him.

'Oh, hi, Jermaine. I didn't see you following me. Where are you going?'

'Wherever you are, madam. Captain's orders. Captain Huntley messaged to say there is an intruder on board and, given your... penchant for finding trouble, he believed it prudent for me to stay by your side.'

I narrowed my eyes at him, getting nothing but an innocent look in return. 'I don't find trouble,' I grumbled. Then I let my shoulders sag as I relented. 'I'll admit it does tend to find me though.' The elevator pinged its arrival, the doors opening to let several people off. The day was warm, and the sun terrace beckoned for most. In contrast to the happy people passing me, I wasn't going to get to work on my tan today.

'Which deck, madam?'

It was a good question. I was so intent on getting to Ensign Gosnell's cabin that it hadn't occurred to me to find out which deck he was on or even to look up a cabin number. Now I was stuck but since I didn't have a universal keycard anyway… 'Let's go back to see Dr Kim. To the infirmary please.'

Blood and Notebooks

'It's the same blood type,' announced Dr Kim. Mentally I performed a fist pump; finally we were getting somewhere. 'You understand that doesn't make it Commander Krill's blood though, right?'

I stared at Dr Kim, my mental fist pump evaporating in a puff of smoke. 'No. I did not know that. Lieutenant Baker said you could test it and tell us if it matched.'

Dr Kim shook his head. 'There are eight different blood types. It's a small number when compared to the seven billion people on the planet.

The blood I just tested is B Positive. It is the third most common blood type, found in about eight percent of the world's population. That makes it common enough for there to be a decent percentage of this ship with the same blood type. This blood could just as well be from the sasquatch over there.' I could hear the enormous chef snoring like a warthog from across the infirmary. This was disappointing. 'What I proposed to do for Lieutenant Baker was show him if it wasn't the same type. That would have ruled Ensign Gosnell out immediately. As it is, all you know is that the blood on his clothing still might have come from Commander Krill.'

Once again I was back to square one. I needed to get into Ensign Gosnell's cabin. There might be nothing of interest in there but I wouldn't know until I looked. I needed something I could use as leverage to make him talk. Otherwise this case might go on forever and that might disrupt some quality gin drinking time.

A flash of inspiration hit me. I didn't need to get a universal door card. I just needed to get his card from his belongings in the brig. I wouldn't even need to dress up like an idiot this time. I thanked Dr Kim for his time, wished him luck with his sleeping sasquatch and tugged Anna in the direction I wanted to go. My feet felt like I was putting in a lot of miles. The Aurelia is basically a floating town with shops and restaurants, cinemas and bars. If one chose to, one could walk all day and never cross the same spot twice. As I went back to the crew elevator to go down to the deck with the brig and then make my way to the brig itself, I racked up another half mile or more.

Ensign Gosnell was presumably in a cell because he wasn't in the interview room when I passed it. I found the tall guard on the brig's reception desk.

'Hello,' I tried as pleasantly as I could. I had Anna in my arms to make myself look extra friendly because I was about to ask to rifle through a man's personal effects and had no authority to do so. 'Can I see Ensign Gosnell's items, please?'

The tall guard smiled. 'Of course, Mrs Fisher. The captain said you were to be given anything you wanted.'

I rolled my eyes, wondering why I ever bothered trying to be devious and put Anna down to free my hands for digging through his wallet. The credit card sized keycard was in the first slot on the left-hand side. 'Do you know his cabin number by any chance?'

I got another smile as he clicked the mouse for the computer next to him and pulled the keyboard within reach. A few clicks and keystrokes later. 'Deck three, Mrs Fisher, room zero, zero, thirteen. Unlucky for some,' he laughed at his own joke and I offered a polite smile as I took the card and left.

'That was easy, madam,' Jermaine commented on our way to the elevator.

'Yes. If only this mystery was. Nothing adds up yet. We may or may not have Commander Krill's murderer in custody and if Ensign Gosnell did murder Commander Krill, not that I have the faintest idea why yet, it doesn't mean he killed Julian Young.'

'They will be able to check the blood in a lab soon though. I am sure the deputy captain, Commander Yusef, will have already contacted the authorities in Malta to arrange evidence to be checked.' Jermaine was right; I was being impatient. The mysteries I have been forced to solve in recent weeks, mostly so I could stay alive, had all been obvious once I saw enough of the puzzle. This time it was different; the puzzle felt like it was alive and kept wriggling around to avoid me grabbing it.

I kept my feelings of defeat to myself, biting my lip as I challenged myself to solve the case before we got to Malta. Arriving at Ensign Gosnell's cabin door, I cricked my neck like I was warming up for a fight, told myself the clue I needed was right behind the door and as Jermaine put the keycard to the panel, I snarled, 'Knock, knock,' just like I had once seen John Wayne do prior to kicking a door in on an old movie. Then I kicked the door as hard as I could with my right foot and bounced off onto the floor as it failed to budge an inch.

Anna licked my nose.

'Are you alright, madam?' asked Jermaine, calmly turning the handle to open the door before offering me a hand to get up. I wanted to say that I had just broken my leg, but I knew I hadn't despite the pain messages my brain was receiving. Jermaine didn't have anything else to say, his expression said it all. So, feeling stupid, I pushed myself off the floor, gritted my teeth as I limped into the cabin and took a seat at Gosnell's desk when Jermaine offered it.

'I'll check the computer, okay?' I said as I settled into the chair. 'Do you want to start searching the room?' At fifty-three, I am almost hopeless with a computer, but my reliable butler kept quiet about that as he began opening drawers.

Anna hopped onto the low bed by climbing first onto a bag. Then she turned around a few times and settled down to sleep. I clicked the mouse, but nothing happened. 'The power button, madam,' prompted Jermaine politely as he moved to the next drawer.

I had to duck my head under the table to find the tower and a button with a power symbol on it. I sat back to wait but still nothing happened. I clicked the mouse again in a hopelessly futile gesture. 'On the wall, madam,' advised Jermaine, his tone still gracious and encouraging.

I scanned around to find a cable and traced it to the wall where it was plugged in but not switched on. I flicked the switch there and waited again. Still nothing. I began to grind my teeth and could feel Jermaine preparing to politely point out what I was doing wrong now. I held up a hand to stay his next comment and checked under the desk again. I had turned on the power at the wall but apparently having pressed the power button on the tower when it was off at the wall meant I hadn't turned it on at all. I tried yet again, vowing to the inanimate object that I was going to throw it against a wall if it continued to defy me.

Finally, the screen made a noise and swam into life.

Then a box appeared in the middle of the screen demanding a password.

This time I muttered something a lady ought not to know the meaning of and grumpily exited the chair. 'Your turn,' I announced.

'Yes, madam,' Jermaine replied calmly as he slid into the seat and began to poke around the desk. I muttered some more about stupid technology and picked up the search where he had left off. A small chest of drawers contained clothing and undergarments but nothing interesting or pertinent to the investigation.

Behind me, as I moved on to start on his bedside cabinets, the computer beeped again and a new screen appeared. 'How did you get past his password?' I asked.

In response he held up a faded yellow Post-It note on which several lines had been crossed out. Only the bottom one was legible. 'Most systems demand the password be changed on a monthly or quarterly basis and people run out of memorable words to use. Everyone I know uses a note somewhere to record their passwords on. This was underneath the keyboard.'

I made a note of his advice, mostly filing away that I could hope to find a password for anyone's computer if I looked about a bit. Of course, if anyone asked how I cracked the password I was going to say I took their birthdate and star sign and then performed duplex Boolean algebra equations in my head in order to work it out, not show them a Post-It note.

As Jermaine scanned through the files and folders, I ran out of drawers to inspect. I looked under the bed but all I found was a sock. I heard a story once about young men and the socks found next to their beds, so I kept my hands away from it and sat back on the carpet to think.

A voice from the recent past came to me. Shane Sussmann, the lame duck of a man who turned out to be a vengeance-fuelled maniac with an axe. Performing this same daft task with him a few weeks ago, he said the murder weapon was always under the chest of drawers. Shrugging to myself, I figured I might as well check it out. Lo and behold, when I lifted the bottom drawer out of the way, I found a treasure trove of things he didn't want anyone else to see.

Not that I thought my find was going to tear the case apart because beneath his bottom drawer was a four-inch-thick pile of vintage Playboy magazines. I lifted one out. It was from July 1978. Was this a gift from his grandfather or something? I thought men just used the internet now. Disappointed again, I put the magazine back but as I picked up the drawer to put it back, I spotted something else. It wasn't just dirty magazines hidden beneath the drawer, there was a little notebook too.

I sat on the bed with it, carefully examining the pages. The notebook contained rows and rows of numbers.

It looked like a handwritten ledger but there were no currency symbols so I couldn't be sure I was looking at monetary values or something else. I turned a few more pages and my hand stopped when I found what looked to be a smoking gun.

'Jermaine, dear, can you take a look at something with me?'

'Of course, madam.' He left the computer chair and took a seat next to me on the bed so he could also examine the small notebook in my hands. On the top of the left-hand page as I held it, the title read, Bursar's overwrite authorisation codes. Beneath it were a series of random alphanumerical codes each with a label to tell me which account they could overwrite. Jermaine said it for me, 'He has the bursar's codes.'

'Only the bursar and his deputy should have these. He stole them from someone, and Julian found out somehow. No.' I shook my head, that wasn't quite right. 'He stole them from the bursar and was using them to steal money. Julian spotted an irregularity in one of the accounts.' I was getting excited now as the picture formed in my head. 'Julian didn't understand what he was looking at, so he asked Gosnell and he arranged to come by his cabin later that day. When he got there, he killed him, altered the accounts to remove the anomaly and wrote the suicide note.'

Jermaine wrinkled his nose. 'Why kill the bursar?'

The fat lightbulb of brilliance above my head fizzled, popped and died. 'Okay. Maybe the bursar found out and threatened to expose him.'

Jermaine thought about that but shook his head again. 'There was already an investigation under way, why didn't the bursar just tell us the killer was Gosnell? Or, if he wasn't sure, just tell you that Gosnell was up to something?'

Why not tell us? Why not tell us? I asked myself on repeat. If the bursar knew or suspected that Gosnell was Julian's killer and then did something that made Gosnell kill him, why not put his hand up and rat him out? 'Because he was being blackmailed?' I tried.

'Yes, madam. That could work. Perhaps Ensign Gosnell caught Commander Krill and Lieutenant Scott and threatened to expose them. Maybe that's how he got the codes.'

I picked up what he was saying. 'Then, having killed Julian Young, the only one that can expose him is the bursar so he waits until Deepa stops watching him, sneaks out and stabs Commander Krill to death in a back alley.'

'Two murders in twenty-four hours. One planned, one spontaneous. Madam, I believe you have it.' I tried the scenario out in my head a few times. The notebook was the smoking gun. Until I found that, I thought the only people who could have overwritten the account file on Julian's computer were the bursar and his deputy. Since it occurred after Julian was killed the same person who overwrote the file was the killer. The bursar acted shifty because he was trying to keep his affair with Lieutenant Scott secret. He had already been blackmailed into giving up sensitive information when he handed over his authorisation codes, so he was going to lose his job and his position and probably his wife if the truth came out. I think he knew that Gosnell killed Julian and he was prepared to keep it quiet for his own reputation.

Sitting on the bed, I could feel the tension in my shoulders dissipating. This had been a hard one. I sat for a moment and had a mental gin and tonic, telling myself I would have a real one just as soon as I presented the evidence and told the story.

After just a couple of minutes, I got up and continued poking around his cabin, just in case something else presented itself – like a big note saying how and why he did it because one of those would be nice. There was nothing though and Jermaine said the computer contained nothing of interest. A forensic computer analyst would undoubtedly go through it as part of the full investigation that would have to happen. My job was largely done though.

Feeling relaxed and satisfied and a little bit spent, my pulse spiked when we heard footsteps approaching at speed down the passageway outside.

Case Closed

Jermaine stood up to his full height and flexed his shoulders while twisting both ways at the waist. Then he stepped over to the door and used it to conceal himself. Whoever came through it was about to get a shock.

'Mrs Fisher,' Deepa Bhukari's voice called out as she rounded the doorframe and looked inside. Jermaine relaxed. 'Lionel said we would find you here.' I gave her a quizzical look. 'That's the tall fellow in the brig,' she supplied. 'Most people call him Lurch.' I could see why.

'Yes. Well, he was right. Here we are.' She stepped into the small cabin, Lieutenant Baker just behind her though he elected to stay outside rather than crowd the small space any further. I held up the notebook. 'We've got him.' To answer their unspoken question, I told them all about the codes and how I thought events most likely played out. We couldn't confirm some of the details because Commander Krill was dead. Shannon Scott might know about the blackmail, but my gut told me she didn't. They would ask her and find out one way or another though it made little difference.

Lieutenant Baker placed the notebook into a small evidence bag and sealed it. Then he indicated for us all to leave and I called for Anna. She was nestled comfortably on the bed but yawned and stretched as she got up. Her route off the bed was the same she used to get up; via a tote bag on the floor. Jumping down, her hind paws caught in the handles to trip her.

'Oh dear,' I commented to myself as I returned to make sure she was alright. The contents of the bag was exposed now and seeing it caught my breath. 'Guys. Come look at this.'

Martin peered over to see what had attracted my interest. The answer was an enormous pile of cash. 'Where did he get that?' The question wasn't aimed at anyone, but it did need answering. It was vital evidence but not something he could fit into an evidence bag. Deepa and Martin would need to return or send someone from the team back while they quizzed Ensign Gosnell. I backed out of the room, Martin locking up after me.

'We should have found this hours ago,' he commented as we walked along the passageway to find an elevator and the way out. 'I should have sent someone to search his room while we conducted the interview.'

Deepa argued with him, 'There were too many other tasks to perform: get all the passengers on board, make sure they are all accounted for, deal with Commander Krill's body, inform his wife that her husband was dead while carefully not revealing the affair he was having because what would be the point. If you wanted to find someone to do the search, there probably wasn't anyone available.' Martin looked like he knew she was right but was berating himself anyway. Deepa wasn't finished though, 'Then there was that business with the paraglider guy.'

I had forgotten him completely. 'Oh, yeah. What happened to him?'

'He still hasn't been found. Schneider is leading one team, but I think they have every available crewmember searching the ship.'

At the elevator, I picked Anna up again. I had an unwarranted fear she would get on and the doors would close or the other way around and she and I would be stuck on different sides when the car inside started moving. She snuggled under my chin affectionately as I squeezed her into me. I had solved the mystery of Julian's death but now there was a new mystery: There was a man on the ship who had stolen on board by flying down to land on the helipad like James Bond. He even sounded like James Bond in his black dinner jacket. I wasn't getting involved though. My day was done. The elevator stopped to let the two lieutenants off; they were going to take the notebook and use it to get a confession from Ensign Gosnell. My theory about how it played out and why he killed Julian and Commander Krill might be wrong on some aspects. I expected that, but they promised to fill me in on the bits I had wrong later.

Arriving back on the passenger decks, Jermaine asked, 'To your suite, madam?'

The sun was high in the sky since it was well into the afternoon now. I had to supress a yawn as I considered what I ought to do with the rest of my day. 'Actually, I think I shall take a cocktail by the pool.' I had a pile of books on my bedside table that had been laughing at my attempts to read them for weeks. Well, one of them was going to get it today.

'Very good, madam. If you let me know when you are returning, I shall draw you a bath.' He was so thoughtful.

Confession

The fruity cocktail I selected was as refreshing as it was strong, the first hit of alcohol from the bottom of the glass almost making my toes curl. After that I used the straw to stir it before taking each sip.

The sun would beat down for another couple of hours and I felt that I deserved the quiet time I was taking. This was, after all, my vacation and a once in a lifetime trip. The book I chose to read was a murder mystery, but I worked out who the killer was on page six and had given up on it by page thirty. I would try another one later. I was content for now to just lie on my sun bed among the happy passengers and watch the world go by. I drifted off to sleep at one point, waking with a snort to find I was drooling onto my swimsuit. The woman opposite me smiled in a way that let me know she had seen me, but that I was no different to anyone else. Anna was tucked into my side, her paws in the air as she too enjoyed the sunshine on her body. She opened an eye to squint at me with her upside-down head, but when I didn't try to move her, she closed it again.

As the sun began to dip, I thought perhaps I should think about moving. Not that it was about to get cold, but I had an evening to fill and could do whatever I wanted. My dinner with

Barbie and Hideki never happened yesterday and my breakfast with Deepa, Martin and Jermaine went sideways this morning before we even ordered coffee. Some company might be nice.

I called Barbie but got no answer. I knew she wasn't working at this hour; she always had the early shift and was in the gym most mornings between five and six o'clock. She had her boyfriend with her though and he was leaving in just a couple of days so they were probably putting their time together to good use.

Failing to reach Barbie, I tried Deepa next. Would she still be working? It would be another long day for her if she was but having been entrusted with a high-profile case, assigned to her by the captain no less, she was most likely going out of her way with Martin Baker to make sure everything was being done correctly.

She answered though. 'Mrs Fisher. How can I help?' Her answer and tone sounded too professional; we were friends now so perhaps someone else was listening. She softened though as she continued speaking. 'Sorry, it's been a long day. Ensign Gosnell still won't talk, he certainly won't confess and the only thing he has said, is that we have it completely wrong.'

'Oh?' I wasn't all that surprised, he acted as if he believed he could just keep denying his crimes until we got bored and let him out.

'Not only that, the chief of police in Athens finally got back to us about the stamp on his hand. It's from a well-known club. It looks like Gosnell was there. We are going to check but it might be that he couldn't have killed Commander Krill because he was there at the time of his murder.'

I was stunned. Not because I got it wrong but because it was now the second time I had pointed the finger at the wrong person. I would wait to hear about the club and whether Gosnell had an alibi, but I already believed it would prove to be the case and was pushing my brain to work out what I had missed. Dinner plans were scuppered already, so I needed to get back to my suite, get dressed and get my sleuthing hat on. This game wasn't finished yet.

'Good evening, madam,' Jermaine's deep voice echoed in my ear as he answered the phone.

'Can you run me that bath please?' I was sweaty from the day and from lazing about in the sun by the pool. This evening might prove busy so I should at least get clean before facing its challenges.

Picturing Jermaine walking slowly across my suite's living area to my bedroom and then slowly around the bed to get to my bathroom and then diligently turning on the taps and adding just the right amount of bath salts, I figured I had just enough time to exercise Anna before it was ready.

A ten-minute saunter in my bikini, sarong, and wedge heels took us to the front of the ship where very few ever go and her favourite spot to err… go. When that task was complete, she yipped at me to get me moving because I had ground to a halt and was staring out to sea.

I was adding up what I had thought to be disconnected parts and trying to figure out what they meant and if they were in fact connected at all. A man had parachuted or paraglided, I didn't know what the difference was, onto the ship earlier just as we were setting off from Athens.

Commander Krill had been murdered in a brutal knife attack in a back street in Athens while on his way to meet his lover who was far, far too attractive to stoop to sleeping with him unless she was being motivated by something other than attraction; like for instance money or preferential treatment.

Then there was a chef who was more bear than man and he had been beaten to a pulp. Finally, there was Ensign Gosnell. He had the Bursar's authorisation codes. What was he doing with them? He wouldn't tell Baker and Bhukari how he got them but there had to be something criminal behind it. He left the ship after going to watch a soccer match and choosing not to stay. He stayed out all night, only returning to the ship the following morning still wearing his clothes from the night before. They had blood on them that might be the bursar's.

I meandered back to my suite, pondering the facts I knew all the way. Inside, I slipped Anna's collar off as I shut the door behind us. It was cooler in my room than outside, the air conditioning convincing me that I really wanted the bath. Jermaine appeared from my bedroom. 'I have set out fresh towels, madam. The bath is exactly ninety degrees Fahrenheit.'

'You're are too much, Jermaine.' I didn't mean it though. I thought everyone should have a Jermaine to look after them. One thing was for certain, I was going to struggle when I got back to England and had to fend for myself again. Not only would I have to get used to a lot less space, given that I was going to have to buy a new place to live and had no income, but also because of little things like I hadn't picked up an iron in over two months now.

Jermaine nodded curtly and left me to my own ministrations, calling Anna as he went as it was her dinner time. She dashed after him, her tail wagging so hard her bum was swinging from side to side.

A short while later she wandered into the bathroom to find me, her claws clicking on the heated tile to announce her approach. I popped my head over the side to look at her and she did the thing again where she looked like she was waiting to read my lips. I silently mouthed the word, "Biscuits," and she barked in excitement, her tail wagging again. I didn't have a biscuit for her but as I laid my head back in the bath, I started going through all the elements of the case again, continually circling back to the belief that there was another layer I hadn't yet worked out. Something to do with what happened to sasquatch the chef.

Suddenly, like a live wire getting dropped into my bathwater, I knew the question I had failed to ask. It hit me like a lightning bolt, startling me into motion. I needed to get moving so I could find out the answer. I had to make a phone call; one I really didn't want to make, and then annoy a few members of the crew for answers they might not want to give.

However, even if I got all the answers I wanted, I had a nasty feeling I was going to have to go back to Athens to prove I was right.

WRONG TURN

I was out of the bath and in my robe in under a minute, Anna trotting along behind me because I was agitated, and she always picked up on my mood. I called out as I towelled my hair dry, 'Jermaine!'

'Yes, madam.' He scared the living daylights out of me, speaking from three feet away where he was checking a vase of flowers and trimming stamens from the lilies in it so they would not fall and stain the carpet. I hadn't seen him as I exited my bedroom with my towel on my head.

I hoped no one was going by outside or they would surely have heard my scream and would, even now, be sending for the guard.

'Are you quite alright, madam?' he asked patiently.

I wanted to hit him with something but there was no time. 'Can you please contact Lieutenants Bhukari and Baker? Please ask them to attend my suite as soon as they are able.' I looked about for my phone, which I spotted on charge near the computer; Jermaine was invaluable. Heading for it, another thought occurred to me. 'You may also want to think about changing. We may have to go back to Athens.'

'Athens?'

I had already pressed dial on my phone so I nodded that I was being serious and waited for the person at the other end to pick up. When he did, I started talking right away, 'Dr Kim, is your patient awake?'

'Who's calling please?'

I almost tutted but caught myself; a panic on my part should not constitute one on his. 'Good evening, Dr Kim. This is Patricia Fisher. I wish to enquire about the consciousness of your patient,' I said with tremendous calm.

'Oh, good evening, Mrs Fisher. Which patient?'

'The enormous damned sasquatch you had to sedate!' I snapped, my impatience getting the better of me. 'Please, Dr Kim. Is he awake or not?'

'Not currently no. The sedative wore off, but he awoke confused and distressed which is not uncommon with concussions. I gave him another shot. Why?' Because I wanted to poke him in the chest and get some answers, that's why. I didn't waste any time saying that though. Instead I just asked his name, wrote it down and disconnected.

Jermaine was just hanging up too. 'They are on their way, madam. Is there anything else I can help you with? Will I need to pack for you?'

'Pack?' My brain was whirring at high speed but engaged in other tasks, so I missed what he was asking to start with.

'Sorry, no. I hope we won't have to go at all, but if we do it will be a short trip. Could you fix me a sandwich or something though, please? I don't think there will be time for dinner.' He gave a curt nod and walked slowly to the kitchen, Anna seeing his trajectory and opting to follow; where there's food, so shall the dog be.

I hurried back to my bedroom to find clothes. If I knew Bhukari and Baker, they were probably running to get here, imagining that I had something juicy for them. Well, I did, and I didn't. Our investigation took a wrong turn right at the very start. At least, that was what I now believed. I just had to prove it to myself and to them and to do that I had to get some answers very quickly.

To get one answer I made the other phone call; the one I didn't want to make.

It rang for a while, threatening to switch to voicemail just as it was picked up. I imagined the person at the other end deliberating whether to answer or not. 'Patricia. It is late. Why are you calling again?'

'Good evening, Charlie. I'm sorry to disturb your evening.' I had to be pleasant if I wanted any help from him. 'I hoped you might be able to spare me a couple of minutes to explain how the pension account for the crew of this ship might work.'

'You want me to explain finance to you? And you want me to do it in just a couple of minutes?' He was being arrogant. Deliberately so because I wanted something from him, and he was a petty person.

'Yes, please,' I replied sweetly. 'Bullet points will do. For instance; if I wanted to borrow a large amount of money from it without anyone else knowing and then put it back later. Could I do that?' For the next five minutes, I listened and made notes so I might understand better what he was telling me. When he finished, I nodded to myself. There was something here. A forensic accountant would be able to find it now that I knew what to look for, but I saw the need to now make yet another phone call. I didn't have a number for the next person on my list though. Nor a name, nor even the certainty they existed. It would prove one way or the other who was guilty and who was not, so I was going to have to work it out.

I thanked Charlie, wished him a good night and disconnected. Research was required to now find the missing information, but I hadn't managed to get dressed yet, so I was still stuffing my legs into my knickers when I heard Anna bark and Jermaine answer the door. My hair was dry and tidy though and I got the swipe of makeup done while I still had the robe on so all I had to do now was throw on the clothes I picked out. A minute later, with my belt between my teeth, I went hopping out through my bedroom door still putting on my shoes as I went. I got three sets of raised eyebrows and a head tilt from Anna. Clearly my haste was making me look a little deranged.

I wasted no time with explanations or greetings. 'The chef's name is Marco Kalinowski. He's still sedated so we need to speak with the master chef.' I nodded my head to draw their attention to the clock. 'However, it's right in the middle of the busiest time of day for the kitchens so I doubt he will want to speak with me. To overcome that, we are going to have to visit him. Do you know where he will be?' Hungrily, I grabbed the sandwich Jermaine was holding on a plate on top of a silver platter and took a large bite while I waited for Deepa or Martin to answer.

Martin reached up to grab his radio. 'It should be easy enough to find out.' He turned away as he pressed his send switch and started talking.

Deepa got my attention. 'Why are we asking about the chef? I thought he was just a guy who got into a fight and lost.'

'That's what I intend to find out. How long will it take you to get changed?'

Martin said, 'Roger. Out.' And turned around to face us again. 'He's currently in the top deck restaurant overseeing the set up for a wedding breakfast being held there tonight.'

'Super. Let's go.' I grabbed their arms and shoved them toward the door. Anna darted forward to get ahead of us. 'Uh-uh, little girl. You need to stay here.'

Jermaine fetched her, deftly scooping her into the air with his right hand while keeping the tray bearing my sandwich upright with his left. I snagged the sandwich on my way out the door and shouted, 'Won't be long,' as it began to swing closed.

I hadn't done anything about getting the missing information though, so I darted back inside leaving Deepa and Martin in the passageway, bewildered by my constant change of direction.

'Is there something you forgot, madam?'

'As a matter of fact, there is. I have a fun task for you while we are out.'

Master Chef

On our way to the upper deck restaurant, which was the closest place on the entire ship the master chef could have possibly been, I did my best to explain why I wanted to talk to him. I don't think I did a good job because neither Deepa nor Martin managed to grasp what I tried to tell them about lipreading.

'Your dog can lipread?' confirmed Baker.

'Yes. Sort of. I think.'

'So, because your dog can lipread, we need to ask the master chef if Marco

Kalinowski has been hurt before?' I gave up at that point and hoped it would become clear when I had some answers. With two of the ship's security team at my side, I was able to waltz directly into the upper deck restaurant even though it was shut off for all guests tonight.

Baker caught the attention of the first chef-looking person we saw. 'Where can we find the master chef?' The man was carefully putting the finishing touches to a hand-carved mermaid on a wave crest. It was made from butter so would get destroyed in seconds when the wedding guests came in. It looked spectacular though. Baker gave him a second to finish what he was doing but was just about to speak again when the man took a step back. Then he turned around, the floppy chefs' hat moving to reveal his face. Baker recognised him. 'Ah, Master Chef, good evening.'

Apparently, we had found him. I hadn't met the man before but felt like shaking his hand because the food on board was exquisite. 'What can I 'elp you with, Lieutenant?' he drawled in a French accent so thick I thought it had to be fake.

'I have a question about Marco Kalinowski,' I said quickly, drawing his attention.

'Oo is Marco... arm sorry, I didn't catch 'is name.'

There was no time for messing about. Every minute we delayed, the Aurelia steamed further and further away from

Athens. I thought a simple description would do the trick. 'The biggest man in the entire ship.'

Recognition dawned. 'Oh, the bear.'

'Yes. You probably do call him that. He is currently in the infirmary,'

'Yes, I know. What of eet?'

'Has he been injured before? In the same way, I mean. Bruises and cuts that make him look like he has been in a fight?'

He raised a haughty eyebrow and pointed to the butter creation with both hands. 'Madam, do ah look like I have time to know the details of all my staff?'

I was getting a twitchy eye from talking to the chef. His accent was atrocious, and his attitude stunk. Biting my tongue,

I asked, 'Who would know? Does he 'ave,' I faked my own French accent, 'a supervisor I could talk to?'

He burst into French in response, throwing his arms in the air as he got upset. I wasn't going anywhere though, and I could do upset too. As his attention swung away from me with another wild gesticulation, I grabbed the front of his immaculate white tunic with both hands. Both Deepa and Martin stepped in to pull me away but not before the master chef squealed in surprise.

'Tell me, or you'll be remaking the mermaid from scratch,' I snarled.

He darted backwards to put himself between me and his sculpture, warding me off with his arms. Then he yelled,

'Eric! Eric! Attend!' The master chef was looking at me like I was a madwoman. Right now, maybe I was.

'Where are you going with this?' Deepa whispered insistently into my ear.

A man I guessed would turn out to be Eric was rushing across the open area of the restaurant. The wild-eyed master chef shouted for him to stop dawdling even though he was already running.

'Yes, Chef?' he asked as he skidded to a stop.

I got in first though. 'Do you know Marco Kalinowski?'

He flicked his attention between his boss and me and back to his boss and back to me. 'The bear? Yeah, he's on my crew. Damned fool got himself beaten up again. For the size of him, you'd think others would be too wary to pick a fight with him.'

He knew what I wanted him to know. That was good enough with me. To the master chef I said, 'We need to borrow this one for a minute.' Eric looked confused about what was happening and why two members of security were here for him. I grabbed his elbow and dragged him to the exit.

'What's going on?' he asked, clearly now concerned he was in some kind of trouble.

Outside, I let him go but manoeuvred around to face him. Deepa and Martin were indulging me thus far but they would stop me if I didn't explain myself soon. 'I just have a couple of questions about Special Rating Marco Kalinowski. That's all. If you can answer them, I promise I will leave you alone.'

He glanced at the security with their uniforms and sidearms and then back at me. 'Yeah. Yeah, okay. What do you want to know?'

'You said he has come to work with injuries consistent with being in a fight before. How often?'

'Oh, err. A few times. He says people pick fights with him because he is so big. That never made sense to me. I tell you what though, it only happens when he hangs out with that pal of his.'

'What pal?' I asked. I was almost vibrating with anticipation now.

'Um. I don't know his name. I've seen them together a few times though. Only when we get to port though or get close to it. His little friend turns up and they go off together and the next thing I know Marco has bruises on his face. I think his little friend has a mouth on him and gets into trouble he can't handle. Then Marco has to save him.'

I was letting it all sink in. 'Lieutenant Baker, do you have a picture of Ensign Gosnell, please?' Martin pulled a handheld tablet from his right trouser side pocket and kicked it into life. Silently he tapped the screen a few times and turned it so Eric could see the screen.

'Yeah! That's him. What's his name?' Eric squinted at the screen to get a look at the name, but Martin put the tablet back into his pocket.

I had all I wanted but gave myself a second to scour my brain; was there anything else I needed to ask? 'Have you noticed Marco to be flush with cash at any point?'

He laughed at the suggestion. 'Marco?' Goodness, no. He's always pleading poverty that one.' I thanked Eric for his time and walked away. 'Hey,' he called after me, 'what's all this about?'

I didn't answer. I couldn't yet even if I wanted to. Part one was complete though; my latest theory had been tested and survived.

On the way back to my suite, Martin caught up with me. 'Mrs Fisher, you are going to have to tell us a little more. What is this about? How is Marco Kalinowski connected to Julian Young's death? Or Commander Krill's? What is going on?'

I smiled at him, aiming for enigmatic but probably just making myself look demented instead. 'Can you fetch the captain? I think we will need him.'

'Fetch the captain,' he echoed, his tone a little sarcastic when he said, 'Yeah, of course. Why not?' He started on his radio again, calling Alistair. I had a request that only he could grant.

Deepa and Martin both wanted answers, both wanted to know more, but I wasn't ready to share yet. I still had answers to gather. Then, when I was sure, I would reveal everything.

Connections

I had to wait for Alistair, but Jermaine had been good enough to turn up the name and number of the person I wanted to call while we were out. I didn't know what this call would reveal, or if my instincts would prove to be off. There was one easy way to find out, so I slipped into my bedroom and dialled the number.

It was answered almost immediately. The voice at the other end not recognising the number but familiar with calls arriving from different international destinations. 'Hello?' It was a woman's voice.

'Good evening. My name is Patricia Fisher. I work for Purple Star Cruise Lines.'

'Oh, my gosh! Has something happened to my husband?'

'No, no, no.' I replied quickly having scared the woman. 'Nothing like that. Actually, this is nothing more than a routine call to make sure we are doing our part in taking care of the families of our crew.'

I heard the woman relax, thankful that I was not calling with terrible news. Then we spent a few minutes chatting and I learned the thing I hoped I wouldn't learn. There was still ambiguity regarding who had done what, even though I now had almost all of the why. With the call completed, there was really only one thing left to do.

Alistair would arrive soon, but until he did, I reclined onto my favourite couch and encouraged Anna to join me. She climbed onto my lap and then climbed me to lick my chin. With that important task complete, she settled and put her head down to sleep although she lifted it again to sniff my drink when Jermaine delivered a stiff gin and tonic. I didn't need the alcohol, but Lady Mary would approve and with her returning, I needed the practice.

Alistair would have dropped what he was doing to see what I wanted so urgently but it still took him almost fifteen minutes to get to me while I fought hard to not tap my foot. Hearing footsteps approach at a hurry, I placed a hand on Anna to keep her still just before the knock came at my door.

Jermaine was, as always, slow to cross the room but finally Alistair was here, and I could hope to get the last answer.

'Good evening, Patricia,' he said with a nod at the others in my cabin. 'Lieutenant Baker said you needed me. I assume this is to do with Julian.'

I nodded. 'Yes, it is.' Okay, I was going to have to word this correctly so that I didn't sound mental. 'Ensign Gosnell was our prime suspect for the murder of the bursar which ought to also make him the prime suspect for Julian's murder. I had thought the bursar killed Julian because he was acting shifty and was one of only two to have the access codes to overwrite the details in the account Julian was working on. That proved to not be the case, but it seems likely that Ensign Gosnell didn't kill the bursar because he was at a club. I want to know what that club is and whether we can prove he was there last night or not. Basically, we are eliminating the possible suspects one by one. The chief of police identified the name of the club for us, but since Ensign Gosnell refuses to tell us anything of use, I am left with only one course of action to determine what part he played in Julian's death.'

I didn't tell anyone about the call I just made. They might feel there was enough evidence to convict and thus deny the request to return to Athens. For me, it was completely necessary; there was a big fat piece of unknown regarding Ensign Gosnell and his bear-sized friend. Until I knew precisely what they were doing, I couldn't close the case. So I had one course of action: we had to go back to Athens. 'Alistair, I need the helicopter.'

My question caught him by surprise. 'Say what now?'

'I have to go back to Athens.'

I had his full attention, that was for sure. 'Good heavens, why, Patricia?'

I put my glass down and got up so I could pace as I tried to explain as much as I needed to explain. 'Marco Kalinowski and Steven Gosnell were up to something. I think I know what it was, but I cannot prove it from here. If I am right about them, then I have been wrong about almost everything else. It will give me the final answer I need in order to reveal Julian's killer. I've got it wrong twice already when my answers all made sense. This time, I have to know for sure.'

The captain stared at me, and for a moment, I thought he was going to deny my request. But he didn't. 'Okay, Patricia. I'll get the pilot there in a few minutes and arrange for a car to meet you at the other end.'

Lieutenant Baker had a question, childishly raising his hand so he could interrupt. 'We've been sailing for hours. What is the range on the helicopter? Or, to put it another way, are we going to get stranded in Greece?'

The captain shook his head. 'We're mostly hugging the coast and going at cruising speed because it's not far to our next stop in Malta and I want to arrive at an appropriate time of the day. I would estimate the helicopter will get you back to Athens in under an hour of flight time. Provided you are not there too long, the comparative distance, because you can fly overland to catch up, will have barely changed.' Having supplied his answer, Alistair also stood up. 'I'll get you that helicopter,' he said as he put his hat back on. Then he focused on me as he was about to move. 'Patricia, might I have a word?'

He was going to warn me to be careful or something, he had that look about him. 'Of course. The others need to get changed anyway.' Looking at Lieutenants Baker and Bhukari, I said, 'Your uniforms will not work for tonight's excursion.' I spoke to Jermaine about his butler's outfit earlier, so all three nodded their acquiescence and exited the room which left Alistair and me alone.

'Are you going to get into more trouble, Patricia?'

A laugh escaped my lips. 'I certainly hope not. You do know that getting into bother is never my intention, right?'

He grimaced. 'Yes. You do know that what you intend never seems to prevent the trouble occurring anyway, right?'

I crossed the few feet that separated us and wrapped him up in my arms. With my head pressing against his chest, I promised to be careful and to call him directly if I got arrested or shot. I said it with a chuckle, but my comments just made him sigh despondently as if I shouldn't joke about something that was likely to happen. Then we kissed and he left me, heading back to run the ship while I ran through a mental checklist to see what else I needed to do.

It was Anna's normal bedtime. In the few hours I was out, the two of us would normally be sleeping, so I felt secure that she would do just that without me here. I tucked her up in her little doggy bed in the corner of my bedroom and made sure she had water. Coming back into the living area, I saw Jermaine emerge from his adjoining cabin. He was wearing his Steed outfit again, complete with umbrella and bowler hat.

He saw me looking and shrugged. 'It feels like an appropriate occasion for its use, madam.'

To tease him, I drawled out my answer, 'Riiiiight.'

'Hey, Patty, what's going on? You look like you are about to go out?' Alistair hadn't shut my door behind him, anticipating that I was about to go out, and now Barbie's head was poking through it. She came through it properly now, pulling Hideki behind her. 'In fact, Jermaine looks like he is dressed for action.' She squinted at me with accusing eyes. 'Are you about to do something crazy and dangerous?'

'Um.'

'Gosh. You are, aren't you?' Now she dragged Hideki fully into my suite. She was dressed for an evening out in a summer dress with her hair pinned up and Hideki wore matching Japanese silk trousers and tunic. They were probably just returning from dinner in one of the restaurants. 'Tell me what it is right now,' she demanded, all excited and bubbling over.

'It's nothing exciting. We need to pop back to Athens. That's all.'

My answer confused her. 'Patty, the ship already sailed, you can't get off now.'

Smiling because she was being a bit blonde for once, I said, 'We're taking the helicopter.' It was the wrong thing to say.

'Oh, my goodness. We are coming with you!'

'We are?' questioned Hideki.

Barbie was bouncing on the spot, excitement giving her nervous energy to burn. 'How many people does the helicopter hold? Is there room for us?

I've never been on a helicopter before. How fast does it go? Will we get to see Athens at night from the air?'

I couldn't help but laugh. 'Okay, okay, crazy woman. You can come, but we are not staying long. We need to visit a club, ask a question, and then get back here.'

Jermaine spoke up to answer the next question before she got to ask it. 'Mrs Fisher believes she has identified Julian Young's killer and the reason for his murder. The trip to Athens is to confirm a few facts before she incarcerates the guilty person.'

Barbie still looked confused. 'But I thought you already caught him. People have been talking about it.'

'I got the wrong guy. Or... I sort of got the wrong guy... I think.'

She wasn't sure what to make of that comment. 'How soon are you going?'

Relative Distance

The answer to Barbie's question turned out to be right now as Deepa and Martin barrelled back through my door. Both were dressed in mostly black, Deepa in skin-tight leggings that showed off her muscular legs and Martin in skinny black jeans above sturdy black outdoor boots. Both wore leather jackets, not that they matched but they looked kind of like a TV cop duo ready to bust some heads.

Six of us did a final check to make sure we had phones and wallets and in Jermaine's case a functioning umbrella. I wasn't sure how long it took to get the helicopter ready, but we hadn't given them much time. A steward appeared at my door as we opened it to leave, startling the poor man as he was just about to knock.

'Mrs Fisher?' he stuttered. 'I was sent to escort you to the helipad. The pilots are waiting.'

'Jolly good.' This was ever so efficient. We accessed it from inside the ship using a staircase hidden behind a door I had never noticed before. I must have walked in front of it a thousand times without questioning where it went. I thought I knew my way to the helipad, since I had been there earlier today during the excitement with the parachuting intruder, who, according to the steward, had still not been caught. The helipad I was on earlier wasn't where the ship's helicopters were kept though. Without the steward to guide us, I might never have found it.

Confusingly, when we reached the top of the stairs and came through a door, the helicopter, emblazoned in Purple Star Cruise Lines livery was inside. I was not the only one to stare at the ceiling above our heads.

'Shouldn't there be some sky to take off into?' asked Barbie, her forehead wrinkling in confusion. To answer her question, the ceiling began to open with a rumble from the hydraulics operating it. Above us the night sky peeked in through an ever-widening gap in the middle.

Then, as the steward stood to one side, a strapping chap in a flight suit opened a side door on the helicopter and jumped down. 'Good evening, everyone. I'm Flight Lieutenant Theodore Mitchell, but everyone just calls me Teddy. The pre-flight checks are done, and we are fully fuelled so hop on in and let's get out of here, yes?'

He was bursting with enthusiasm which, when I thought about it, was probably because they were getting to take the helicopter somewhere. In over two months on board I had seen it move only half a dozen times and it was always for some superrich gazillionaire who wanted a private flight to somewhere. This was going to be more exciting for the pilots than that.

We did as instructed and piled into the aircraft, each of us buzzing with our own excitement. Teddy made sure everyone was strapped in, chatting amiably about the aircraft safety record and its capabilities in case anyone was worried. When he got to me, he knelt one knee on the floor to bring his head down to my height. 'I understand you have a car meeting you when we land. We will land at a private airstrip owned by the city police; those are my instructions anyway. How long do you anticipate being in Athens?'

It was hard to estimate how long it might take us because I wasn't sure what the distance was from the airstrip to the club or what traffic might be like in an ancient Greek city in the middle of the evening. Nevertheless, I guessed and said, 'Maybe an hour or a little more.'

Nodding at my answer he fixed me with a serious look for the first time. 'Try to keep to that if you can. The Aurelia is heading away from us all the time. It will take us an hour to get there and land. If you are much more than two hours, the ship will be too far away to catch up.'

Martin interrupted with a question I wanted to ask, 'The captain said you would be able to go overland to get to the ship and that the comparative distance would have barely changed. Is that not right?'

Teddy smiled. 'No, it's not. Like most sailors, the captain failed to take into account the contour of the land when he looked at the distance involved. He sees a straight line from Athens to the ship; I see mountains we have to go around.'

'Can't you go over them?' asked Deepa.

This time Teddy shook his head. 'Too high. The air up there gets thin and we get no lift. Trust me on this: we have to go around. It won't be a problem if you can keep to your timeframe and get back to us in two hours.'

With the warning delivered, Teddy took a final look about the cabin before taking his seat in the cockpit. There were headsets for each us of so we could talk during the flight because the noise from the engines was otherwise deafening. We soon discovered he was not exaggerating as they started up.

Five minutes later, with some final checks completed and the roof fully open above us, the helicopter lifted gracefully into the sky. The view as we left the Aurelia was spectacular enough to distract me from the sensation of flying in such a small aircraft. Though it was necessary, I didn't like it and would be glad when it was over. Most everyone stared out of the windows as we set off, the great ship the only source of illumination in an otherwise inky black sea.

Settling back into my seat and closing my eyes to minimise the nausea I felt, I considered Teddy's warning: two hours. Two hours or we get stranded and getting back then becomes a pain. I only needed to get inside the club and ask a couple of very simple questions. Two hours was far more time than we needed.

At least that's what I thought.

Athens by Night

I must have dozed off at some point because a squeal from Barbie brought me awake with a start. As my eyes flashed open, the pilot pitched the aircraft to the right and swooped downward. Oh my, goodness! We were being attacked again!

Barbie's laughter then rang in my ear and the pilot said, 'That's the Parthenon on your right now. If I level off, you should be able to get a good look at it. Across to the left…' He was giving everyone a quick guided tour of the city from the air, making it exciting for them and for himself no doubt as he performed a few minor aerial acrobatics.

I gripped my chair and tried not to spoil everyone's fun by vomiting. The landing strip was just ahead he announced, reminding us again that we needed to be back within a couple of hours if we didn't want the journey back to the ship to be problematic. His parting comment as I mercifully departed the plane was, 'We can have a better look at the city on the way back if you like. Assuming you get back in time. Next time I'll make it exciting.' My stomach churned over again. I was not a fan of flying in a helicopter.

I managed to pat his arm in gratitude for the offer but if there was time to see the city from the air later, I was going to veto it. My feet were back on solid ground so now it was time to find the club. Now, I don't know whether it would prove to be a good thing or a bad thing, but the car the cruise line sent for us was a huge, shiny, black, stretch limousine. We all fit inside it and still had room for more.

'To club Denaides, please,' I said when the driver asked us where we wanted to go.

He used the intercom to speak to us but when he got my answer, the heavily tinted screen dividing back and front powered down to reveal his concerned face. 'You want to go to club Denaides? Are you sure, madam?'

'Quite sure, thank you. We have a tight time frame too, so if you could... step on it a bit. That would be helpful.'

He didn't step on it though. 'Madam, do you know what club Denaides is?'

I gave him the honest answer. 'No. Not really. Please feel free to enlighten me, but I do need to go there, and I wasn't joking about needing to be quick about it.' He opened his mouth again but closed it when I lifted a finger of warning. 'Drive, please,' I insisted, my voice soft though I tried to impart my impatience with it.

The driver shrugged and swivelled around in his seat. He was muttering to himself in Greek as the window powered up to cut off his voice. Once we were moving, I pressed the intercom button. 'You wanted to tell us about the club? I assume it has a nefarious reputation?'

'Nefarious? I'm not sure what that means, madam, but it is not a nice place. Many people get hurt there.'

Barbie shot me a worried look. 'Should we be going, Patty?'

She had every right to ask. 'I have to. You might want to stay in the car. I shouldn't worry too much about me though; I have two armed guards and two ninjas to keep me safe. Besides, I only need to be there a few minutes.'

Barbie put her hands on her hips as she gave me a level stare. 'Okay, Patty, it's time to spill. I'm happy to be in Athens and the flight was so much fun but you look to be walking into yet another trouble spot and I think we ought to know why.'

I could hardly present an argument. Especially since she was right. So, to distract them from the driver's word of warning, I told them what I believed Marco the sasquatch and Ensign Gosnell had been up to and how that had led to Julian's death. No one said a single word until I finished.

As I sat back into my chair, having leaned forward to engage them while I told the tale, Martin Baker stared at me in fascination. 'How on earth did you work that out?'

I smiled my best attempt at an enigmatic smile and said, 'My dog can lipread.' I was getting good at being cryptic. He didn't get a chance to challenge me on that because the car stopped.

We had arrived. Outside the left side windows of the plush limousine was a rundown looking place with a neon sign above it. The neon sign was broken so only part of it illuminated. The letters that did work spelled out D-E-A-D. It was not a good omen.

'Well this is lovely,' murmured Deepa as she got out of the car.

The driver was holding the door and not looking happy. 'Madam, are you quite sure I cannot take you somewhere else?

There are so many nicer places to find entertainment than this.'

I didn't doubt that he was right, and truth be told; I really didn't want to go through with my plan now that I had seen the place. We had come all this way though, so I was going in even if no one else came with me. 'Can you wait here? We won't be long.'

A snort of laughter escaped his lips at my request. 'Madam, if I even attempt to wait here, the car will be stolen and me with it before you can return. I shall be waiting a short distance away. Call this number when you want me to return.' He handed me a small card with a number written beneath his name.

I slipped it into my handbag. 'Thank you, Anatoly. We will not be long,' I repeated a statement I hoped would be true.

Twenty minutes of our two-hour window had been used up already. Like it or not, it was time to do it or chicken out and go home. As Anatoly pulled away with a spray of gravel to mark his haste, I saw that Barbie was with us.

'I thought you were going to stay with the car?'

She shrugged. 'I think I would be more nervous not knowing what was going on. Besides, it's been almost a day since I last got arrested and almost a week since someone tried to kill me.' She was smiling, but her joke was too accurate to be funny.

Deepa, also impatient to get it done, started toward the club, turning and walking backwards as she said, 'At least the limousine made us look like high-rollers.'

We were being watched by more than two dozen men but none of them approached us or bothered us as we came near the club's entrance. They were hanging around outside the club, talking and smoking and making it look even less inviting. There were also two ugly and unpleasant looking doormen blocking our path and neither attempted to move as I expected them to when we got to them. Neither had a smile going spare either.

'Members only,' said the one on the left, raising a hand to stop us. He had a crew cut that showed off a scar running all the way across the top of his head and a crooked nose that suggested it had been broken many times.

Not allowing myself to be put off, I smiled and said, 'We have money enough to pay for membership.'

The first doorman's colleague added his own voice. 'No. Membership has to be earned.'

Now I was getting irked. 'Okay, so what must we do to earn membership?'

Our eyes swung back to the first doorman as he looked me up and down. 'You do not qualify. He turned his attention to the rest of my party, scrutinising each one in turn. 'He can try, if he wishes. If he succeeds, you can enter as his guests.' He was pointing to Jermaine and I had a nasty feeling that I now knew what the price of earning membership was.

Jermaine stepped forward but met my arm as it came up to stop him. I wasn't waiting outside while he went in alone. No way. I tried a different approach. 'There was a man here yesterday.' I looked at Martin, prompting him to show them the tablet with Ensign Gosnell's picture on it. 'He would have had a much bigger man with him. A man they call the bear. I need to ask a few questions about them, and I am willing to pay for the answers.'

'No. No questions,' snapped doorman number one. His tone and expression assuring me that his decision on the matter was final. Some of the men who had been watching us were now moving inwards to close a semicircle around us.

It was time to leave.

'Madam, perhaps I should...'

'No, Jermaine.' He was going to suggest that he go inside, do their test and qualify as a member. The answer was always going to be no. 'There'll be another way. Let's move,' I hissed at the team. They were all relieved to be moving away from the club.

They were that is until I told them my new plan.

No One Talks About Fight Club

Once we had retreated far enough for them to no longer be able to see us and thus lose interest, I began to circle around. 'It has to have fire exits, right?'

'You want to break in, Mrs Fisher,' confirmed Lieutenant Baker, sounding less than comfortable with the concept.

'No. Of course not. I want to pay for entry like a normal person and go inside. Since that option is not on the table, I am left with having to break in.' He said several rude words and kicked the wall.

It was Hideki who came to my rescue just when I thought I was going to have to do it alone. 'Fire exits won't work; they are designed to be solid and don't even have a handle on the outside. What we need is the gents' toilet.' Everyone looked at him. 'In a building this old the toilet will be against the outer wall. The windows always end up getting opened because of the smell.'

Deepa looked at him with a questioning face. 'That doesn't happen in the ladies.'

'Maybe not. Guys, am I right?'

'He's not lying,' conceded Martin.

Hideki nodded his thanks. 'So we need to find the toilets. I go in through the window and open the first door I come to. You can walk in without anyone knowing anything is amiss.'

'Won't the exits be alarmed?' asked Barbie.

I shook my head. 'Not in a building this old.'

It didn't take us long to find the toilets. The waste ventilation pipe sticking up above the roofline gave its location away, and Hideki was right about the window and about the smell. However, the window was almost six feet off the ground necessitating a boost from Jermaine to get him there. He waited for a lull in toilet traffic and slipped inside leaving the rest of us in a dark alleyway.

There was a nondescript door further up the alleyway which had no handle on the outside. All we could do now was wait to see if it was that one he opened. Just enough time passed that I started to worry he might have been caught, but with a clunk and then a creak, the door swung outwards and Hideki's face shone in the moonlight.

Barbie clapped as she scooted over to slip by him with a kiss. The rest of us followed, sneaking down a dark passageway inside as we followed the roaring noise of an excited crowd. Turning a corner gave us our first view of the club's inside and its patrons. Those I could see were all facing the other way so no one saw us join the crowd but looking between the heads I could see what they were all looking at and I had my answer.

I was right. It was a fight club and Ensign Gosnell had been here with his large Russian friend. It explained Marco's injuries and it explained the bag of cash we found in Ensign Gosnell's cabin.

My feet stopped at the back of the crowd, but my friends were weaving their way between the back row to get a better view. I thought it ill-advised but since it had been my force of will that dragged them here, it was only fair that I let them take a quick look.

The centre of the large room was filled by a steel cage. The size of a boxing ring, its four walls were made from a steel that looked borrowed from an old-style jail cell and they reached up twelve feet into the air. There was a door on one side for access and egress. Just as I saw it, the smaller of the two bareknuckle boxers inside the cage, hit the other with a punch to his jaw that threw a spray of blood and saliva into the baying crowd and knocked him out. The referee was outside the ring, a fact which should give anyone an indication of the brutality of the matches. He performed a ten count, declared the man still standing the winner and asked if he wanted to continue for another bout as two men entered through the small door to carry the victor's unconscious opponent out.

Next to me, a man leaned toward his friend so he could speak. There was so much noise in the room, he had to shout to be heard which meant I also heard him. 'Boring tonight, don't you think?'

He spoke English!

I tugged at the elbow of his shirt to get his attention. His head spun around to see who was there and then down when he realised the person behind him was smaller than expected. 'Hello,' I said with a smile. 'Can you explain how this works. I'm here with my boyfriend but he spotted someone he knew and left me here. It's my first time and I don't understand the bit about staying on for another fight.'

The hard look his face wore when he swung around had softened as soon as he saw it was a woman tugging at his shirt. Now he seemed only too happy to fill me in. I guessed from his accent that he was American, but I couldn't place where from. Texas maybe or Oklahoma; Barbie would know but it wasn't important. Like everyone else here, his face bore scars from fighting. 'Well, little lady, I'll tell you, it's real simple. A fella can put himself forward for a fight. If he wins, he gets a prize purse, but people bet on the fights and the fighter can also bet on himself. He can never bet against himself though. If they ever suspect anyone of rigging a fight, well I tell you, those fellas don't tend to ever come back.'

'What about fighting more than one fight?' I asked, on a roll now and building up to the big questions.

'Well, that's the best part. It can really build the tension. If a fella thinks he is tough enough, he can bet that he will win two, or more fights. He has to decide on a number and he doesn't get to see who his opponents are in advance so, I'll tell you, that fella has to really think he is tough.'

'Does anyone ever do that?'

'Sure. It happens a lot because that's where fellas can win big. There was a guy in here last night; biggest man I ever saw. He bet he could win ten straight fights. He even had a promoter fella with him, getting the crowd going and betting on his own man. He came with a pile of cash too and he was laying down crazy bets. Ten fights in a row; no one had ever even attempted that. Then, when the crowd are going nuts and getting excited, his promoter throws in that for his last fight, the big fella will take on not one, not two, but three other fellas at the same time.' I was dumbfounded by what I was hearing, but the man had more to tell me. 'It was incredible, but he did it. He looked like hell afterwards, but that little promoter fella; he cleaned up. I don't know how much money those two made but I lost every penny I bet. I'm here tonight to make a little of it back.'

I had heard enough. There was no longer any doubt about what Ensign Gosnell had been doing and only minor conjecture about the rest of it. It was time to go.

As my new friend faced the other way to look at the cage in anticipation of the next bout, I managed to attract Barbie's attention. She nudged the others and they all made their way back to me, their eyes widening as they came closer though, all of them looking my way but focused on something behind me.

Feeling a presence to my rear, I hesitantly turned around and there was doormen number one smiling down at me. 'Hello, I am Alekos Alexandrakis, the owner of this fine establishment. I warned you not to come in. Now you have to qualify to be a member.'

How to Earn Membership

I swallowed down my fear and stared defiantly up at his ugly broken nose. 'What does that entail?' I demanded to know, doing my best to keep my voice from wobbling.

My informative friend leaned across. 'I thought you were here with your boyfriend. This is members and guests only.'

'You have to fight,' Alekos said with a smile. Jermaine stepped forward to protect me, bringing his body between mine and the dangerous looking doorman. 'It seems we have a volunteer,' he announced with a chuckle. Looking Jermaine up and down, he nodded. 'I tell you what. Because I like a woman with a bit of fire, I'll let you all off with just one of you fighting. He has to win though.'

'Only winners qualify as members,' chipped in my chatty friend.

Then Hideki stepped forward. 'I will fight.'

Jermaine frowned as he turned his attention to the smaller man. 'You are skilled, Hideki, but it is my task to protect Mrs Fisher.'

'That may be so,' Hideki countered. 'But we are all in this. My skills are superior to yours. All that muscle makes you slow.'

'I'm not slow,' gasped Jermaine, looking genuinely hurt by the suggestion.

The doorman watched the back and forth like it was a tennis match, smiling the whole time but eventually calling, 'Stop! This is easily settled. You will both fight as a tag team.'

'You said just one,' I protested.

He gave me a shrug and pointed to Jermaine and Hideki. 'Who am I to deny either of them? They are both so keen.' Then he leaned backwards a little to speak with a man standing close behind. 'Find Gustav and Sven. They will provide the crowd with great entertainment.' Lifting both arms in the air to get the crowds' attention, he bellowed like an announcer, 'Our next match will be a tag team event with the Kirov brothers, Gustav and Sven, on one side and on the other I give you Black Steed...' Jermaine frowned at him as he tried to decide whether to be insulted or not, 'and the son of Jackie Chan.' His roar echoed across the room, igniting excitement. To get them to bet he shouted. 'I'm putting ten thousand on the newcomers. Who wants to win big with me tonight?'

'Jackie Chan is Chinese,' Hideki pointed out. 'I'm from Japan.'

Alekos shrugged. 'No one cares.' As the frenzy to place bets started, Alekos looked at me. 'The bout starts in five minutes. Get your champions ready.'

'What if we refuse?' I defied him.

He lifted a single index finger. In reaction to his silent signal, three men each side of him opened their jackets to reveal heavy calibre machine guns. 'I don't advise that course of action,' he replied calmly.

As he walked away with his entourage following, we all formed into a quick huddle. 'What are we going to do?' squeaked Barbie.

Hideki answered, 'I'm going to qualify as a member of this club, babe.'

'Me too,' added Jermaine, the pair of them each trying to out-macho the other.

'Neither of you has to do anything,' I argued. 'We can call the police. No one has to get beaten up.'

Martin shook his head. 'I don't think this is the sort of place the police try to raid.'

'So, what are you saying?' I was getting a very bad feeling in my middle. I had brought my friends into this and now there was no way out without at least two of them getting hurt. 'There's no way out without a fight?'

Grimly Martin nodded, but where he looked worried and I felt sick with terror, Jermaine and Hideki looked positively enthralled.

In the cage, the announcer was warming up the crowd again and inviting Gustav and Sven to the ring. Through the crowd on the other side of the room, I could see two heads poking out above everyone else's as the two men made their way to the cage. The Kirov brothers were huge. Not huge like Marco the bear, but either one was twenty percent heavier than Jermaine and a couple of inches taller and they had to be twice the size of Hideki.

Barbie grabbed her man's arm. 'No!' she wailed, but Hideki gave her a gentle kiss on her cheek then forced her grip open so he could also start toward the cage. The crowd parted to let him through.

'Would you mind holding this for me, madam?' asked Jermaine, handing me his hat, umbrella, and jacket. I felt positively sick, but it was fight time.

As they neared the entrance to the cage, I started thinking in terms of our recovery plan. Once the Kirov brothers did their damage, I hoped we would be permitted to leave. If their injuries were not life threatening, we would head to the helicopter and get back to the ship. They could be treated and cared for there. Any worse, or any suspicion that they might be worse, and we would go directly to a hospital. As a plan it was rubbish. I needed something more solid; something I could rely on. As the guys made their way to the cage, I took out my phone, backed up a few paces and made a phone call. I had yet another request for Alistair. He really wasn't going to like this one though.

The volume of the crowd picked up as the announcer explained the rules. There weren't many. It was full-contact, bareknuckle fighting. A fighter could tag in a partner at any point and the new fighter would enter the ring. This could only happen if the fighter tagging out was able to leave the ring of their own accord. There would be no two on one fighting. When a fighter lost, the remaining fighter from that pair had to defeat both fighters from the opposing pair. One at a time, but still both of them. The only way to lose was to quit or be knocked out. Looking at the crowd baying for more blood, if Hideki or Jermaine quit before they were deemed to be beaten, it might go even worse for them.

Tag Team

I don't know how it was decided, but Hideki was going first. The cage door closed with him and one of the Kirov brothers inside it. The announcer told us it was elder brother Gustav, then counted down and rang a bell to start the fight.

Gustav raised his fists and rolled his shoulders, hamming it up a bit for the crowd as he circled the smaller man. Hideki looked serenely calm standing in the centre of the ring, his arms loose at his sides and his knees slightly flexed as he watched his opponent.

Ten or fifteen seconds ticked by before, either through boredom or frustration, Gustav switched direction and darted in with a huge haymaker punch. Hideki moved so fast I barely saw it. Barbie was turned away from the fight, unable to watch with her head buried in my shoulder. So, she missed her boyfriend demonstrating his speed and skill.

Gustav's punch sailed harmlessly by Hideki's face and carried on when it hit thin air and Gustav realised he had lost his balance. As the big man pitched forward, Hideki leapt into the air, landing a hard kick to Gustav's right kidney. It caused him to sprawl across the canvass. The crowd, who had been cheering and howling suddenly fell silent. Hideki's leap and kick pitched him high into the air. As Gustav hit the floor of the cage, Hideki reached the apex of his upward trajectory and began to come back down, falling to earth with a killer grimace twisting his face.

He landed on Gustav's back, wrapped the man's head up in both his arms and held on tight. The younger Kirov brother had been sharing a joke with the man next to him as he lounged with disinterest against the outer cage wall. Now he was staring with disbelief as Hideki's choke hold robbed Gustav of the oxygen supply to his brain. In less than ten seconds after the first punch was thrown, the fight was over.

Sven was outraged, but tag team rules allowed him access to the cage now and he wasted no time. Hideki stood back, regaining his feet and preparing to face the other brother. A shout stopped both men. 'Hey! No fair! It's my turn.' Jermaine was holding out his hand to be tagged.

I couldn't believe this.

The crowd were still silent but as Hideki walked reluctantly across the cage to swap with my butler, they started cheering for Sven again. Alekos's tactic had worked. By placing a large bet against the obvious favourites, he enticed everyone else to bet against him. There was a big pot of money to be won and no one wanted Sven to lose. Not even Alekos with his huge bet because the mood of the crowd suggested they might take the place apart if this went against them.

Sven waited in the ring for Jermaine to get in it and for the cage door to close, but he wasted no further time after that. My butler looked very out of place in this environment. The fighters and spectators were mostly in jeans, heavy work boots and vests. In contrast, Jermaine's lower half was clothed in a pair of tailored black trousers with a thin pink pinstripe and a pair of well-polished black brogues. His top half was in a white shirt though he had rolled the sleeves up. The trousers were held up by bright red braces and he wore a black bow tie.

Had his brother not gone down so easily, I believe Sven would have been playing to the crowd and making a big thing of his opponents clothing. As it was, he knew he had to beat Jermaine and then Hideki, so he was being cautious.

It didn't help him. Sven was a giant bruiser of a man and undoubtedly used to street fighting, but I knew Jermaine to have some very particular skills which had been honed by years in various dojos. Sven stepped in to deliver his attack the moment his opponent was in the cage, but Jermaine pounced forward. He took the leading punch early, removing all the power from it, then gripped Sven's arm in both hands to roll it around against the wrist joint.

Beside me, Barbie was cheering and whooping which was drawing unwanted attention our way. Angry faces in the crowd knew they were about to lose their money and wanted someone to blame. We made easy targets. With my focus on the faces now looking our way, I missed Jermaine doing whatever he was doing but I heard the ten count and the announcer's voice saying the match was over. Our boys had won their fight but we were not out of trouble, we were just getting into it.

'Ringers!' someone shouted. Then another voice claimed, 'It's a fix!' I spotted Alekos making a hasty exit before anyone saw him which left the crowd with no one to fixate on but us.

A shot rang out, the suddenness of it and the boom of noise made me jump, but it came from right beside me. 'Everybody, back off,' insisted Deepa Bhukari. Martin had his sidearm out too, both taking them from holsters under their jackets.

The corridor we came in through was still right behind us, just a few yards away but we needed Hideki and Jermaine. The guns were keeping everyone at bay, but it wouldn't be long before people at the back thought to use the drinks in their hands as projectiles. Mercifully, the boys were shoving their way through the crowd to get to us, striking out when necessary to make the space they needed.

'Start backing up,' Martin instructed, tugging at my arm as he took a step back. When the boys joined us, he yelled, 'Now run!' Barbie had hold of my hand and we ran along the dark corridor, almost missing the turn to get back to the fire exit but barrelled along it to get outside. Behind us, Martin and Deepa fired a few more warning shots into the air and soon ran to catch up with us, the sound of the angry crowd following.

When they came through the door and back into the alleyway outside, the rest of us were ready to shove it closed, slamming the heavy door in the face of the first row. My sense of safety lasted about half a second, the bubble bursting as the door opened again and I remembered that fire exits open from the inside.

Car Chase

Jermaine slammed into the door again, forcing it back to almost closed but there were a lot of people on the other side of it. Too many for us to keep them from getting out.

Deepa yelled, ‘Find a car!’ as she drew her weapon again. Aiming high, she put a round through the very top of the door. The shoving from the other side stopped, but the lull wouldn’t last long.

Leaving Martin and Deepa to continue to dissuade the crowd inside from leaving the club, four of us ran around to the car park at the front to find a way to escape.

It wasn't a good move.

Not all the angry mob inside had followed us down the corridor to the fire exit; half of them were coming out the club's main door. In general, they looked despondent. Until the first of them spotted me, pointed, yelled and started running our way.

Barbie squealed, I almost wet myself, but Jermaine's shout caught my attention. He was grabbing my arm and dragging me behind him as he ran. We needed to run alright, but I doubted we could outrun the horde for very long. Too panicked to be able to think of a way out of our latest mess, the blast of a car horn still drew my eyes. It was the limousine! Jermaine must have seen it approaching because he was taking me on an intersecting path.

I didn't know how Anatoly knew to come for us, but my heart leapt at the hope of escape. With gazelle like legs, Barbie got there first, yanking open the door so we could all pile inside, Jermaine more or less grabbing my collar and belt to throw me in like a large bag. The tyres squealed as the limousine shot forward, Barbie leaning through the partition to direct Anatoly to find Deepa and Martin.

Hideki opened the door and hung out of it, shouting to get their attention. Martin saw us first, fear, then relief, crossing his face once he worked out what he was seeing. His shout snapped Deepa's head around just as she fired another shot to keep the horde inside. It was her last though, the weapon's action stopping to the rear with a distinctive sound the crowd inside must have heard because they chose the next second to burst forth.

She was running. Martin was running, a few yards ahead of her and gesticulating madly for us to not slow down. He dived through the door as we drew level, timing it perfectly but Deepa wasn't going to make it. Not at our current pace. Slowing down was going to be dangerous though; cars were already racing out of the car park at the front of the club and the horde coming through the fire exit looked ready to kill.

Deepa got to the road as the car swept ahead of her. She was level with the back of the car and clearly looking for a handhold. Anatoly checked his mirror and slowed enough for her to reach the door. Barbie swung out, caught her arm and once the two of them had their forearms interlocked, she tensed her back and yanked Deepa inside.

Anatoly's foot was already hard on the gas pedal before the door was closed. We had a small lead; but our car resembled a barge, weighed several tons, and was not going to outrun anyone. Smaller cars bore down on us, their headlights filling our rear view. The road was narrow with no way of passing but I knew from the outbound journey that the road widened as we neared the airstrip. When we reached that they could get alongside us, and in front of us, and then they could force the limousine off the road.

He was holding them off for now; five minutes flashed by at high speed as he powered down the single-track road back toward the airstrip. We were getting close to it, but the angry mob was right on his tail, their horns a cacophony of noise from behind.

'Come on, where are you?' I raged, looking about as I tried to spot what I already expected to see.

Anatoly flew through an intersection, coming back into a more commercial area and the road widened as I knew it would. Now the chasing pack could use their greater acceleration and better handling to out manoeuvre us. We were going to run out of time soon, but we didn't have more than a couple of miles to go.

'What are you looking for, Patty?' squeaked Barbie breathlessly.

I didn't answer right away, I was too busy staring out the front window. 'There!' I pointed. 'Drive straight at that and don't let anything get in front of you!'

Anatoly squinted into the darkness. Ahead of us the road went up a small incline and then disappeared as it crested the top and went back down again. A faint glow could be seen coming from the other side.

'What is it?' murmured Barbie.

One of the chasing pack hit the back of the limousine with a hard thunk. It jolted the entire car, throwing us around in our seats and for a second the back end of the giant car began to slip sideways. At this speed, we only needed to come around a few more degrees and it would barrel roll. Anatoly wrestled the steering wheel, pumping the clutch and brake as he steered into the skid. It slowed the car, so as he brought us back under control and we all released our held breaths, the chasing pack were suddenly either side of us.

We were nearly there though, the limousine already going up the incline and the glow of lights in the darkness on the other side now identifiable.

Everyone else saw it too. The police were there waiting for us.

Worried that we might be followed or chased or just need to drive fast to get back in time, I had called Alistair from the club. I told him we were successful and left out the bit about the guys having to fight. However, I asked him to get hold of the chief of police yet again. He had already spoken to him to arrange us using the airstrip, now I needed him to mobilise a battalion of cops so that, if we were being pursued, we could get to the airstrip and escape. Without them, we might have got back to the helicopter but would never have been able to board it.

Anatoly kept his foot down as he breached the apex of the incline and we went airborne. A half second of weightlessness that felt like much longer before we returned to earth with a crunch that loosened my fillings.

A sea of police cars faced us though, three-hundred yards to our front with their strobe lights flashing. The angry mob saw them too, immediately hitting their brakes or swerving as we swept onwards to the sound of cars crashing into each other.

'Wow!' gasped Martin, looking out the rear window now as car after car came over the rise, left the ground and could do nothing about the crash they faced because in front of them were stationary cars that had already crashed. As the giant pile up built and built, Anatoly slowed to a pace that felt less like warp speed and passed between the police cars to arrive serenely at the airstrip.

He let the limousine glide to a stop, then closed his eyes and crossed himself as he said a prayer. Teddy waved to us as he climbed out of the helicopter, his cheerful smile still in place though his eyes looked worried. 'You'd better hurry, ladies and gents. We are way over the two hours.'

The rotors of the chopper were already turning, though not quite at full speed, his need to leave forcing proactivity on his part. Two minutes later, once I hugged Anatoly and thanked him several times, we were in the air and heading back to the ship. There was no time for sightseeing; he acted as if we were cutting it really fine.

And the Killer is...

Unlike the trip to Athens, I stayed awake all the way back. Partly I was still wired; my body pumped full of adrenalin after our escape from Athens, partly it was my overactive brain running through the case again and again as I tried to find a hole in my theory. Mostly though, I was trying to look through the cockpit to see the ship. We had gone over the two hours Teddy said we could afford, and I wasn't going to relax until I spotted the lights of the giant cruise ship in the water ahead.

My neck was beginning to ache. I had to strain it to see around the pilot's seat and still keep my bum in my seat where it felt a modicum of safety. It only took us an hour to get from the ship to Athens, but we had been on our way back to it for more than two hours already.

The pilots were in communication with the ship and had its position. Teddy's voice came over the headsets several times, telling us it wasn't far now. He had clearly been lying the first time he said it, and the second. After the fourth time, I started to worry.

Straining my neck and squinting my eyes as I searched for the ship, I noticed a red light staring to blink on the console between the pilots. 'What's that?' I asked, forgetting to keep the concern from my voice so now everyone else was staring at it too.

'It's, ah. It's the low fuel warning light,' Teddy stuttered.

'Low fuel!' I blurted. Oh, my gosh, we were going to crash into the ocean like Glen Miller and never be heard of again. 'I thought you were going to refuel at the airstrip.'

'That was the plan, Mrs Fisher. They were waiting for an overdue delivery and couldn't spare us any.'

'And you didn't think it was important enough to bring up until now?' Terror was causing me to rant.

Calmly, he replied, 'There seemed little point. There being nothing we could do about it.'

I told myself to be calm, but the terrified part of me growled at the calm part and made it run away. 'How far can we go before the helicopter falls out of the sky and how far to get to a piece of land we can set down on?' I hadn't seen land in a long time so we had to be way out to sea.

'Oh, we would never be able to get back to land,' said Teddy cheerily. 'How about if we just land on that big ship over there instead?'

The six of us in the back all strained our heads to look and there it was, a glowing, beautiful wedge powering its way across the ocean. My home. The Aurelia.

It came closer and closer, Teddy quickly covering the remaining distance though my heartrate didn't slow until we were above it and I could be certain we were safe. I felt like saying a prayer when the helicopter's wheels touched down.

'Welcome home everyone. Please ensure you have all your personal belongings with you before you depart the aircraft and be sure to tip your waitress.' Teddy was annoyingly upbeat. I felt like using a stun gun on him.
In the cockpit he was flicking switches and putting the parking brake on or whatever it is you do with a helicopter. I could hear the engine noise decreasing

but then it got much louder as a person outside opened the door for us to get out and louder still as we all took our headsets off.

Then I spotted Alistair. He was waiting just beyond the edge of the helipad, the wash from the rotors whipping his hair about as it would mine the moment I stepped outside. Jermaine got out and offered me his hand, his first thought always seemed to be me.

Seeing the fatigue on my face, he asked, 'Shall we finish this and get to bed, madam? The day has been long.' He wasn't wrong about that. Using both hands to stop my hair from becoming a bird's nest, I ran for the edge of the helipad. Alistair waited for me, took my arm and all of us, Jermaine, Alistair, me and everyone else escaped back into the calm and tranquillity of the ship.

Now that he wouldn't have to shout to be heard, Alistair said, 'Welcome back, Patricia. I assume you still want to speak to everyone now?'

I had messaged him from Athens just as the helicopter took off, asking him to assemble everyone involved. He was personally invested because this all started with the death of his nephew and I knew he was keen to tell his sister they had caught the person responsible.

He led us to a meeting room on deck five. Since everyone involved was crew and someone was about to go to the brig, it made sense to assemble in the crew area. No one spoke as we went into the room, the persons already there being guarded by half a dozen members of the ship's security team and none of them in a chatty mood.

Upon seeing the captain, one man jumped to his feet. 'Captain, I really must protest. I have been roused from my bed and placed in this room without any explanation. I demand...'

'Demand?' Alistair repeated, his voice hard.

'I think I have a right,' blustered Lieutenant Commander Pilar Singh.

Huffing out a breath through his nose as he did his best to keep his emotions in check, Alistair stepped into his subordinate's personal space. 'You will get your explanation right now. Please take a seat.' Clearly annoyed, the deputy bursar sat back down in his chair and glared at anyone who dared to make eye contact with him.

In the room was every member of the bursary team, most of them looking confused and only half awake. Only one other person was present, beyond myself and all my friends who elected to tag along because they felt invested and needed to hear the end of the story. That person was Marco Kalinowski, the giant Russian.

Most of them were staring at me but then pretty much everyone on the ship, whether crew or passenger, knew who

I was and what I was famous for. Supressing a yawn, I started talking, 'There is more than one crime here. More than one person involved in the two deaths we have witnessed. I will start with the bursar, Commander Krill. Commander Krill was having an affair with Lieutenant Shannon Scott.' A series of gasps went around the room as almost everyone turned to face her. Her cheeks turned an interesting shade, but I moved on. 'I believe her part in that was motivated by the opportunity to do less work. By leveraging her superior, she was guaranteed a good report, which would lead to promotion ahead of her peers, but she also got to shirk a lot of the work which should have been assigned to her. In this, she and Commander Krill had one thing in common: laziness. Commander Krill had either grown lazy or had advanced despite it. He was so lazy in fact that he couldn't be bothered to conduct the authority oversight work that only he and his deputy were authorised to do.' I got another gasp. 'This should not come as a shock. I believe many of you were given access codes by him to do your own authority oversight and sign off on them. What he forgot was that this also meant you had the ability to fudge your figures and overwrite them with the right figures to make it seem like money that wasn't there, actually was.'

'You have to be kidding,' insisted the deputy bursar.

I flicked an eyebrow at him but continued unabated. 'Given this power, none of you thought to abuse it.' I let that statement hang for a few seconds, before adding, 'Except one. Ensign Steven Gosnell is something of an entrepreneur. He sees opportunities and pursues them.' Ensign Gosnell acknowledged the statement as if I was praising him. I looked across the room to the corner where Marco Kalinowski sat. 'You will have noticed the person in the room who is not a member of your team. He is Special Rating Marco Kalinowski and he is a chef. He is also a very capable fighter.' Ensign Gosnell's confident smile slipped for the first time. 'For the last few months, Ensign Gosnell has been entering his large friend into bareknuckle boxing competitions. Last night, while the bursar was being murdered, Kalinowski and Gosnell were at a tournament in Athens where they won a lot of money. Unfortunately, the money he used to bet on his own fighter was embezzled funds from the ship's pension pot.' At this point I turned to my friends so I could explain something to them. 'You might expect that the pension fund is controlled centrally back at Purple Star Lines headquarters, but the transient nature of this vessel and the constantly shifting exchange rates as you move around, mean that it is more stable to extract the money from your wages here. It is probably then exchanged at a more favourable rate in one lump sum at a set point of the year.

That piece of detail is unimportant.' I was using the information Charlie gave me and wanted to move on quickly in case someone asked me a technical question.

'What is important?' asked a small voice near the front of the room.

I looked down to see Annette, the plain girl with the crush on Julian. With kind eyes, I said, 'The important bit is that when Julian joined your team, there was no vacant set of accounts to give him, so the bursar took accounts from many of you. I'm sure this was welcome in most cases because it meant less work. For Ensign Gosnell though, it meant trouble. He was a week away from the biggest score of his life using funds he had taken from the pension fund which was now being scrutinised by the newest and keenest member of the team. I don't think it took Julian long to discover the irregularity. He didn't report it though.'

'Why not?' asked Lieutenant Bhukari, clearly confused now as I was making it sound like Ensign Gosnell was the killer after all.

'We can never know that, but I believe he chose to wait until he was sure about what he was looking at. The next piece of the puzzle was the hardest to work out. It came to me when I was watching my dog and the way she looks at me to see facial cues because she doesn't understand words. Julian lipread. He was very good at it in fact. So good one might hardly know he was deaf at all. It came with some great advantages.'

'Such as?' asked Lieutenant Commander Singh, sounding bored.

'I'm glad you asked, Pil.'

'Pilar, please, if you must address me by my first name.'

'Yes, of course, Pilar. Do you think others refer to you by your full name? Or might they abbreviate it?' He gave me a curious look but didn't answer. He had no idea what I was talking about and no one else could see what I was trying to tell them. 'One of the advantages of lipreading is that a person can do it across a crowded room. They don't have to hear what is being said, so a private conversation in a noisy room, where the two people having it might think they cannot be overheard, is not so private after all.' There was silence in the room as they waited for me to arrive at my point. 'There's one thing about lipreading though: some letters are easy to get wrong. Bs and Ps are especially difficult to tell apart. This is not usually a problem in a sentence or if the letter is hidden in a long word, but if you all now silently say Bill and Pil, you will observe that the movement your lips make is exactly the same. This is what cost Julian his life.' Looking at the faces of the people listening to me, I could see no one had got it yet.

'Ensign Young followed Ensign Gosnell because the pension account had been his and he was therefore the most likely person to have been fiddling the numbers. Julian most likely wanted to be sure about who to point the finger at before he started making waves. It was still his first week on board, after all. He watched a conversation between Gosnell and Kalinowski in which he saw repeated use of the word Bill. He assumed they meant Commander William Krill and that implicated the bursar as complicit in the crime of embezzlement which he suspected Gosnell to be guilty of. Gosnell is guilty.' The young ensign started to argue but I held up a finger to silence him. 'He didn't kill to protect his secret though. I also thought the bursar to be the guilty party until he was murdered and I discovered his authority codes in a notebook hidden in Ensign Gosnell's cabin. The bursar wasn't guilty though, not of embezzling funds or of killing anyone and the name Julian thought Gosnell was saying wasn't Bill at all. It was Pil because that's what they call you, Lieutenant Commander. Ensign Young, believing the bursar was in on it, went to the next person in the chain of command, Lieutenant Commander Pilar Singh and told him the pensions account was being embezzled from.'

'I have no idea what you are talking about.' the deputy bursar snapped. 'Ensign Young never came to me.'

'Then why did you kill him?' I asked calmly.

Lieutenant Commander Singh laughed heartily. 'He committed suicide. You are a foolish woman who has in the past stumbled onto some truth and now believes herself to be some kind of super sleuth. I have no idea why that poor boy took his own life, but I had nothing to do with it.'

I pursed my lips and nodded. 'You knew all about Ensign Gosnell's embezzling, didn't you? Whether it was your idea, or you caught him and then saw an opportunity to take the money you needed doesn't matter. You might even have intended to put it back like I believe Ensign Gosnell would have, but you knew that if anyone got caught, you could say that Ensign Gosnell was the guilty one, he had embezzled and then used the bursar's codes to hide it. As deputy bursar you had equal access to every account.' I looked around the room. I could tell I had it right from the sickened faces Ensign Gosnell and Lieutenant Commander Singh wore. There was more I needed to explain yet. 'When Ensign Young came to you, he voiced his suspicions and you knew there was no way out, no chance that you could take it off his hands and bury it. So you agreed to meet him later to review the evidence with him in private. Did you congratulate him on his diligence?' I met Singh's eyes but didn't wait for an answer. 'I spoke with your wife, you see. She was very happy to talk about the miraculous funding that an anonymous donor had put forward.

She expects your child to make a full recovery once he gets the operation he needs.' I saw the pain in his eyes. A tear ran down his cheek as his face crumbled. 'I was never blessed with children so I cannot say what I would do for them. I hope your son makes a full recovery and I hope you can find a way to explain why another person had to die in order that he might live.'

The captain nodded his head at the security team. They took three men into custody, each guilty of a different crime and each facing a spell in jail. Marco the bear would get the most lenient sentence, he was only guilty by association with Ensign Gosnell but his days with the cruise line were over; bareknuckle fighting was not illegal, but his employers would not condone it either.

Alistair then addressed the remaining members of the bursary team, 'The rest of you are free to go. I thank you for your patience here tonight. There will be repercussions and a full audit will be conducted as soon as a team can be dispatched from headquarters. If you have anything you wish to... identify before it is found, soon would be a good time to do that.'

'Who's in charge now?' asked little Annette. With both the bursar and his deputy gone and Lieutenant Scott suspended, they had no leadership.

Alistair considered the question. 'I will appoint someone as acting bursar in the morning.' With her question answered, they started to file out. I yawned deeply, using a hand to cover my mouth but very much wishing I was already in bed.

Lieutenant Bhukari walked over to me. 'Mrs Fisher, what about the bursar? Who killed him?'

I found it interesting that after my summation, no one else had thought to ask. 'I don't know. It wasn't Gosnell or Kalinowski because they were both at club Denaides. We have a thousand or more witnesses that can place them there. We also know it wasn't Lieutenant Commander Singh because you were watching him. I think he really was mugged. Killed for the few bucks in his wallet in an Athens back alley because he wanted to meet with Shannon Scott and they made sure to pick a place well out of the way. We might never know.'

As Bhukari drifted away, heading for the door and her own bed, Alistair put a hand on my shoulder. 'Thank you, Patricia. Thank you for catching Julian's killer. You are an amazing woman.' I took his hand and kissed it then held it to my face.

'I have to get to bed,' I managed around another yawn that threatened to split my face. Jermaine was waiting patiently by the door even though he had to be equally tired. I clapped Alistair on his arm. 'Go run your ship. I'll see you tomorrow, yes?'

'Yes, indeed. I very much look forward to it.' Tomorrow morning the Aurelia was due to dock in Valetta, Malta and he was taking two days, almost the whole time we were there, to be my companion. We were booked into a hotel and for two days we could act like a couple on holiday without all the distractions his role as captain created. I was looking forward to it as well.

He kissed me goodnight and left me to return to my suite with Jermaine at my side. On the way there, a thought occurred to me. Leaning against the side of the elevator because I felt shattered, I asked my butler, 'Any idea if they caught the parachute guy?'

JAMES BOND

This was not the first time I had walked into my bedroom and found someone in there. In fact, it happened so often I should be getting used to it. As my heart restarted and I leaned a shaking hand against my dressing table for support, I said, 'Who are you and what do you want?'

The immaculately dressed man was in his late thirties, a few speckles of grey around his temples betraying his age but he looked fit and capable and above all dangerous. On my bed, in easy reach of his hands from the chair he was sitting in, was a handgun fitted with a silencer. I doubted he was here to kill me though or he would have done it already.

'Good evening, Mrs Fisher. I apologise for startling you. It was necessary that I remain hidden. There are people looking for me and they have tracked me here. They are on board even now though I wish to reassure you that they will not find me here.'

'How can you be so sure?'

'Because they are looking for me elsewhere. The ship is too vast for them to search cabin by cabin. They will position themselves centrally and wait for me to attempt to get off the ship.'

I pulled out the dressing table chair and sat down. 'Okay. That fails to answer either of my questions though. Should I repeat them?'

This time he smiled at me. 'Your reputation as a tenacious woman is well earned, I see. My name is Justin Metcalf-Howe the second. I work for British Intelligence.'

'Like James Bond?' I questioned.

He inclined his head slightly and smiled. 'Just like James Bond. Though without the constant lineup of gorgeous naked women,' he sighed. 'I have in my possession, the plans for a weapon. The team of scientists who developed it in secret, were not as clever as they thought, and word of their discovery leaked. By the time I got to them, they were already dead, but I tracked the

Chinese agents that took their data and stole it back.' He reached into his left breast pocket and produced from it a thumb drive. 'This is encrypted and protected, so I cannot load it to a computer and send it. The only place it can be read is waiting for me in London. My cover has been compromised though. The Chinese and others are watching for me, but I have arranged for a courier to collect it in Malta.' He leaned forward to place the thumb drive on my bed and picked up his gun. He slid the weapon back inside his jacket. 'Mrs Fisher, your government needs your help. I make no exaggeration when I say millions of lives depend on this information reaching England safely. Take this to my contact in Malta, he will take it the rest of the way.'

I stared at the tiny data storage device. 'Why me?'

He flipped his eyebrows. 'Because you will get the job done, Mrs Fisher. That much I am certain of. I saw the coverage of your escapade in Zangrabar; I know you will see the task to its conclusion.'

'What are you going to do?'

'Lead those watching me on a wild goose chase. They will follow me, thinking I have the data, leaving you to take the data to my contact unchallenged. There is no risk, Mrs Fisher; I would never place you in any danger.' Then he stood up and put out his hand for me to shake.

'God bless you, Mrs Fisher. Your country will soon owe you a debt of gratitude.'

'Wait,' I protested. 'I'm not sure I can do this. I don't know anything about being a spy. I'm just an ordinary middle-aged woman from England.'

He scoffed at my comment. 'Mrs Fisher, there is nothing ordinary about you.'

Then I noticed the dark stain on the chair. I squinted at it as my brain told me what I was seeing. 'You're hurt. You're bleeding!' On the chair by the bed, the soft pastel pink fabric was stained where his right kidney would have been.

'It's no more than a scratch, Mrs Fisher, and not the first time I have ever been shot.'

'You were shot!'

'I must go, Mrs Fisher. My contact will be waiting for you at 1400hrs in the Rumbla Club on Old Mint Street. He'll be wearing a black trilby hat with a peacock tail feather in it and carrying a paperback copy of Catch 22. When you approach him, you must give him a code phrase to identify yourself. You need to remember this. Are you ready?'

I couldn't stop shaking my head. How on earth was I being asked to do this? My country needed me? Surely there was someone more qualified for the task on board this ship. 'I... I, ah. What?'

'Mrs Fisher, this is important.' He winced and as I looked at his face, I saw how pale he was.

I reached for my phone. 'We need to get the doctor to see you.'

He grabbed both my shoulders, gripping them hard to make sure he had my attention. 'There's no time. When you dock tomorrow, go to the Rumbla Club on Old Mint Street. Look for the man in the black trilby and say exactly these words: "I hope the barman here can make a decent banana daiquiri." Have you got that?'

I nodded. 'I hope the barman here can make a decent banana daiquiri.'

'Good. His response will be: "Bananas are out of season. Try the strawberry instead." As he let go of my shoulders and started toward my bedroom door again, my head swam with confusion.

'Good luck, Mrs Fisher. I doubt you will need it. 1400hrs sharp, don't be late, no matter what the reason. Too much is riding on this.' Then, at the door, he paused. 'Oops, almost forgot.' Then in three purposeful strides, he crossed to my nightstand and opened the top drawer. Anna's head popped out. 'She was rather disturbed by my presence in your bedroom. A real fighter that one. I'm glad you don't have a Rottweiler.'

Then, without another word, he was gone. Anna leapt from the drawer to my bed and crossed it to sniff the thumb drive. I picked it up before she could chew it. Bewildered, I wandered back out to my living area to check if he had left. The main door to my suite was locked, but the patio door to the sun terrace was open, the curtain billowing lightly on the breeze. I stared over the edge of the ship wondering how anyone could come and go this way without falling into the ocean. There was no sign of him though, just a spot of blood on the deck to show his passing.

I closed the patio door behind me and meandered back to my bedroom. The thumb drive was still in my hand and I stared at it as I sat on the edge of my bed.

Tomorrow morning when the Aurelia docked in Valetta, I was supposed to be going ashore with Alistair. He and I planned intimate couple time, walking the ancient city and finding a secluded spot for lunch. Now I was going to have to come up with a reason to ditch him and go in search of the British spy's contact.

As I flopped backwards onto the bed and felt Anna snuggle into my side, I asked myself, not for the first time, how I got myself into so much trouble.

The End

Note from the Author

Hi there,

I want to take a moment to share a few words about life as an author. Though I started writing for pleasure at a very early age and won my first award when aged just ten, I never saw it as I viable career. It possibly could have been though and might have saved me from the war disability pension the government sends me each month.

Having finally committed to finishing a novel in 2011, it still took me five years to finish and another to exhaust myself looking for a literary agent. Self-publishing my work has been a joy though also a slog and having quit my horrible corporate soul-sucking job to do this full time, I am working more hours than ever before. The stories queuing in my head are now flowing onto the page faster than ever which will undoubtedly result in the opportunity to take my foot off the gas in due course. I look forward to that, as does my wife, but I am certainly not complaining.

Mostly, when not writing, I think about how I am no longer stuck stationary in traffic somewhere or spending yet another night alone in a hotel in a foreign country. I think airport lounges were the worst – I doubt I could count the hours I spent waiting for flights.

So, life as an author? Well, it's great. Yes, I am working hard and putting in lots of hours, but they are all voluntary. I love what I do and hope that you enjoy what comes out of it. I need a cup of tea now, my four-year-old son is about to arrive home from pre-school so I have a window of opportunity to play with him. I'll pick up the current work in progress again after he is in bed, probably writing into the small hours once again as I smile at Patricia's expense.

Patricia adventures are not my first series though; there are many other books already waiting for you. So, if you enjoy Patricia's adventures, you may wish to check out **Tempest Michaels**, **Amanda Harper** and **Jane Butterworth**. Like Patricia, they solve mysteries and their stories are written to make you laugh and keep you turning pages when you really ought to be going to sleep.

What's Next for Patricia

The Maltese Parrot

When she finds a wounded member of British Intelligence in her bedroom, Patricia really isn't that surprised. I mean, it happens all the time, doesn't it? However, she is surprised, and really not delighted, to hear that he has a secret task for her - find his contact, hand over a harmless looking data storage device that just happens to have the details of a superweapon on it, and save the world from certain disaster. Her country needs her. Well, that's just perfect. Throw into the mix a missing grandmother who just might have been grabbed by sex traffickers, foreign agents who all want the weapon, and the return of her gin-guzzling friend Lady Mary Bostihill-Swank and her relaxing, romantic stop in Malta might be the most exciting two days of her life. Get ready for another cozy thrill ride as Patricia, Barbie, Jermaine, and more get in and out of trouble in an ancient island paradise.

Free Books and More

Want to see what else I have written? Go to my website.

https://stevehiggsbooks.com/

Or sign up to my newsletter where you will get sneak peaks, exclusive giveaways, behind the scenes content, and more. Plus, you'll be notified of Fan Pricing events when they occur and get exclusive offers from other authors because all UF writers are automatically friends.

Copy the link carefully into your web browser.

https://stevehiggsbooks.com/newsletter/

Prefer social media? Join my thriving Facebook community.

Want to join the inner circle where you can keep up to date with everything? This is a free group on Facebook where you can hang out with likeminded individuals and enjoy discussing my books. There is cake too (but only if you bring it).

https://www.facebook.com/groups/115
1907108277718

About the Author

At school, the author was mostly disinterested in every subject except creative writing, for which, at age ten, he won his first award. However, calling it his first award suggests that there have been more, which there have not. Accolades may come but, in the meantime, he is having a ball writing mystery stories and crime thrillers and claims to have more than a hundred books forming an unruly queue in his head as they clamour to get out. He lives in the south-east corner of England with a duo of lazy sausage dogs. Surrounded by rolling hills, brooding castles, and vineyards, he doubts he will ever leave, the beer is just too good.

Printed in the USA
CPSIA information can be obtained
at www.ICGtesting.com
LVHW040807301023
762491LV00003B/8